Devlin planted his hand on the woodwork above Michelle's head, delighting in the way her whole body tensed at the action.

"I don't know what you mean." But it was apparent to them both that she did.

"It's obvious to me, as I'm sure it is to you, that you can use my help. So, if it isn't the nature of my work you object to, then you must take exception to me personally."

"Oh, no, I..." Her voice trailed away into breathy silence as his finger slid down, stroking the length of her cheek.

"What do you have against me, Michelle? Is it my appearance?" He wondered at the color that flooded her cheeks.

"Mr. Rhett, I don't think—"

"What don't you think, Michelle?"

"I don't think we should be standing...so close."

Then, before she could warn him against such an action, he erased the inches that separated them and placed his lips on hers.

ABOUT THE AUTHOR

Popular historical author Lisa Bingham made a smashing debut onto the contemporary scene with *Nanny Jake*, an October 1995 American Romance. She's written nine historical novels and is currently at work on her fourth American Romance. Lisa is recently married and spends her spare time refurbishing her home located in the farmland of northern Utah. Writing is a passion with her, and she enjoys the opportunities it gives her to meet new and fascinating people.

Books by Lisa Bingham

HARLEQUIN AMERICAN ROMANCE
602—NANNY JAKE

THE BUTLER &
THE BACHELORETTE

Lisa
Bingham

Harlequin Books

TORONTO • NEW YORK • LONDON
AMSTERDAM • PARIS • SYDNEY • HAMBURG
STOCKHOLM • ATHENS • TOKYO • MILAN
MADRID • WARSAW • BUDAPEST • AUCKLAND

ISBN 0-373-16635-4

THE BUTLER & THE BACHELORETTE

Copyright © 1996 by Lisa Bingham Rampton

Chapter One

"Madam Worthington will see you now."

Devlin Rhett shifted away from the huge picture window. For ten minutes, he'd been impatiently staring through the glass overlook of Maude Worthington's exclusive penthouse apartment. From here, she had a marvelous view of Central Park—as well as two teenagers with shaved heads who were indulging in a game of leapfrog down the center of the outer sidewalk.

A reaction as familiar as breathing began to tighten the muscles of his stomach as he gave them one final, irritated glance. As far as he could figure, something happened to a child between the ages of twelve and thirteen. They completely mutated, becoming alien beings with temperaments ranging somewhere from the Marquis de Sade's to Bozo the Clown's. How anyone could live through the ordeal of having one of his own, he didn't know.

"Sir?" Wilson spoke again, adding a discreet clearing of his throat.

Shaking himself away from the scene below, Devlin pulled his thoughts back to the matter at hand. There were no teenagers lurking on his professional *or* personal horizon, so why waste emotional energy on the pair in the street?

"You're looking as good as ever today, Wilson."

The butler—who was at least eighty years old and as emotional as a block of wood—didn't even crack a smile.

"Thank you, sir."

"I suppose she keeps you hopping." Devlin had thought his choice of words would at least cause a lift of the brow, but Wilson remained completely stoic.

"Yes, sir. As you say, sir."

Realizing that any further conversation was doomed to such succinct answers, Devlin lapsed into silence, eyeing the man's impeccable attire. The dark suit, starched white shirt and slender tie put Devlin's faded army fatigues to shame. And the shine of Wilson's shoes made Devlin wonder if his own boots were leaving dusty footprints on the immaculate carpet.

Normally, Devlin would have taken the time to change into something more appropriate. But after two hours of practice on an outdoor shooting range, he'd received an urgent message from Maude Worthington. And since Devlin had developed a fondness for the old gal, such a summons had brought him directly here.

Acting on impulse, Devlin hooked Wilson around the elbow, bringing him to a halt.

The old man looked down at Devlin's hand as if he'd never encountered such a situation before. But when he met Devlin's gaze, it was with a placid air of patience.

"Yes, sir?"

"Is something wrong, Wilson? From the tone of Maude's note, I can tell she's very upset."

"It isn't for me to say, sir."

Of course it wasn't, but just once, Devlin would like the old man to show some sort of excitement, anxiety, anger, anything. The very least he could do was sweat—especially since the Indian summer they were experiencing at the moment made it feel more like July than mid-September.

Wilson cast another glance at Devlin's hand, so he released the man, regarding the old gentleman with utmost pity.

"It's ninety-two degrees outside, Wilson. Don't you think Madam will let you loosen the tie a bit?"

Wilson's somber face didn't even twitch. "There's no need, sir. We've been blessed with central air."

The tongue-in-cheek witticism was so unexpected that Devlin was the one tamping down the smile just as the butler threw open the ornate double doors to the sitting room and announced, "Mr. Rhett, Madam."

From the moment Devlin was admitted into Maude's inner sanctum and the panels were closed behind him, there was no more time to wonder about poor Wilson or the archaic life-style he was forced to perpetuate. As always, Maude Worthington took center stage—the woman, the room, the very aura around her assaulting his senses like a slap in the face.

Entering the sitting room was like walking into a bottle of Pepto-Bismol. Everything was pink. The carpet, the draperies, the walls. A pink brocade settee faced a pink-striped swooning couch, while a pale pink marble coffee table had been situated between them, already laden with a pink porcelain tea set and ribbon sandwiches with pale pink filling.

In the center of it all, like the perfect bud displayed in the midst of a dozen roses, was one of the most flamboyant women he'd ever encountered. Maude Worthington, ex-Broadway star, socialite, and world traveler.

She had arranged herself in the middle of an overstuffed divan—which was pink, of course—and the numerous diamonds on her fingers sparkled as she gestured for him to come closer. Her slight body had been draped in a blush-colored negligee ensemble, with ostrich feathers at the wrists and neckline. A bit of the same fluff peeked at him from the mules encasing her slender feet, and her face was framed by a bejeweled pink turban. Even the nasty-tempered Pekingese dog in her lap had been adorned with pink barrettes and a pink, diamond-covered collar.

"Devlin, darling!" she exclaimed, holding her arms wide as if he were some long-lost relative instead of an intermittent employee.

He knew she wanted him to bend for some sort of airy kiss aimed in the general direction of his cheek, but Devlin wasn't in the mood for such social gestures. Not after he'd been yanked off the pistol range by such a panicky message. Looking at Maude now, at the way she was so comfortably ensconced among the pillows, he was beginning to realize the note had been nothing more than a ploy to get him here as quickly as possible.

"Hello, Maude." He sank into one of the seats, glaring in her direction in a manner that he hoped was off-putting.

But Maude merely clapped her hands in delight. "How commando-ish you look, dearest. Is this for my benefit?"

"I was on the shooting range when your note was delivered."

She ignored his steely tone and shivered in something akin to delight. "You were shooting your guns." She wriggled her shoulders as if she'd just been submerged in a particularly stimulating bubble bath. "I simply adore a man with a gun. I do. I really do."

Devlin fought the urge to roll his eyes. He knew she was being completely sincere—which was a frightening thought in its own right. But even though she hadn't graced the stage since the Kennedy administration, she'd maintained her flair for drama.

"Now don't pout, Devlin darling. I know it was naughty of me to summon you so hastily, but I had to do it. I really did."

"What do you want, Maude?"

"There's no need to get so huffy." Her pansy-colored eyes brightened. "I bet you haven't eaten yet, have you? Men always get so gruff and grumbly when they haven't eaten." Her voice adopted that itsy-bitsy-spider kind of tone that adults foisted on children in strollers. "You just sit back and relax and I'll pour you some tea."

Devlin despised tea, but he didn't bother to inform Maude of such a fact. Again. She knew very well that he hated the stuff—she'd even confessed once that she didn't imbibe in anything stronger than the herbal varieties. But ever since her London tour in the mid-fifties, when Maude had determined it was a charming custom, she'd kept it up.

Accepting the fact that Maude would approach the crisis at hand in her own good time, Devlin leaned toward the rose-covered china tea set, which had been placed in the middle of the table. Ignoring the stack of plates, he grabbed a handful of the delicate, crustless sandwiches and began to eat them with a gusto that made Maude grimace.

"You haven't been feeding yourself proper meals, have you, sweetie?"

"I haven't had time."

"You've got to make time."

He shrugged. It was an argument they'd had on a dozen occasions. Since Devlin had served as her bodyguard on and off for over six years, Maude felt it her duty to return the favor and act like some benevolent godmother.

"Shall I pour you some tea?"

"No."

She frowned in disappointment at his implacable reply, but didn't bother to argue. "I'll just have Wilson bring something else, then."

Maude jiggled a tiny silver bell. Within seconds, Wilson appeared in the doorway, making Devlin wonder if the old servant had broken some land-speed record to get there.

"Yes, Madam."

"Will you bring Devlin some coffee or—"

"Beer."

Maude's nose wrinkled in distaste. "Beer, then."

"Very well, Madam."

The door closed and Maude's lips pursed together. "It's not the healthiest choice, you know."

"So sue me."

She sighed and made a waving gesture with her hands, as if shooing his bad mood away. Then, leaning forward with effortless grace, she poured herself a cup of tea, added enough sugar to bring it to the consistency of syrup, then a dash of milk.

Leaning back in her chair, she blew on the steaming liquid. "So, Devlin, dear, did you look at the papers I sent your way?"

She had finally come to the point of his summons.

Devlin nodded. "It looks like a simple enough case. Because of his diplomatic duties, your ex-husband is involved in some delicate trade negotiations."

She huffed in indignation. "He's arbitrating an agreement over coffee beans, for heaven's sake—hardly a thrilling venture." She grew grim. "Who would have thought such an activity could turn violent?"

"Nevertheless, he's had some threats against you and your daughter. Judging by the folder you've sent me, you decided to take the attempts at coercion seriously."

She sipped her tea, grimaced, and put the cup back on the table. "Yes. Ordinarily, I would have ignored the whole affair and chalked it up to one of Gerald's fits of self-importance. But there have been some incidents..."

Devlin grew immediately alert. "Incidents?"

She pushed aside his concern with a negligent gesture. "There's no need to worry yourself. I can take care of myself this time. I've already decided to leave New York for a few weeks. I'll find some quaint little hidey-hole and catch up on my reading. But my daughter is quite another matter. She'll need a bodyguard."

"I'll immediately assign one of my staff members to—"

"No, Devlin," she stated firmly. "I want *you* to see to her safety."

The thread of iron in her voice could not be mistaken, and it caused him to pause. Until she'd sent him the file nearly a week ago, Devlin hadn't even known that Maude *had* a daughter. Not wanting to pry into her personal affairs, he'd naturally assumed that the relationship between them was far from amicable. But judging by the fierce expression on Maude's face, if that was the case, it wasn't because of Maude. It was obvious that she was genuinely concerned about her daughter's safety. So much so that she'd summoned him here this afternoon.

Devlin straightened in his seat, brushing the crumbs from his hands. "You think that's necessary?"

"Yes. My daughter is very stubborn and very proud. As you have probably deduced, my contact with her is sporadic. Whenever I appear on her doorstep, she assumes I'm there to interfere."

"What about her relationship with her father?"

Maude's expression was as mischievous as a child's. "That, I'm pleased to say, is an even worse situation." She offered him a cat-that-got-the-canary grin. "That's why Gerald was forced to handle the matter by informing me first. Michelle won't even speak to him."

"Why not?"

"Because my daughter took it into her head to study psychology and sociology at some of the finest universities in the country. Then, rather than becoming a professor or researcher, she dared to put it to practical use and sank her inheritance into piloting a foster-care program for troubled youth."

"Your husband didn't approve?"

Her smile grew coy. "My *ex*-husband was furious. He's quite the snob."

"What about you? What did you think about such a venture?"

She shrugged. "I don't really care what she does as long as she's happy."

Devlin thought about the situation for several seconds, then reluctantly nodded. "I think I can rearrange my schedule." It would take some doing, but Maude had been more than a good customer, she'd been a good friend.

Maude clapped her hands. "Marvelous! I'll have Wilson pick up the necessary things right away."

Something about the way she said the statement made his eyes narrow. "Things?"

"Yes, of course. You did understand that I wish you to complete this project without her knowing you're there as a bodyguard?"

"I gathered as much, but what does Wilson have to do with such an arrangement?"

"Well, you're a little old to masquerade as a troubled teen—"

"Teen? What the hell does any of this have to do with troubled teens?"

"Didn't I tell you? That's her job. She works with troubled teens."

"Oh, no. No, no, no." He jumped to his feet. "I just spent three months of hell with a teenage rock star, making sure he didn't self-destruct during his tour. I will not—*not*—have anything to do with any human being between the ages of thirteen and thirty."

But even as his tirade was building steam, he caught the way Maude's chin had begun to tremble, her eyes to fill with tears.

"Don't look at me that way," Devlin said, thrusting an accusing finger in her direction. "I don't believe it. Not one bit. You're an actress for hell's sake."

But the tears didn't ease and when she removed a handkerchief from her pocket, he was undone. It was like watching his own mother cry.

Sighing in exasperation, he growled, "All right. I'll do it."

The change in her expression was immediate, and she beamed at him in approval. "I'm so glad. Since you will be working undercover, so to speak, I've already taken the liberty of seeing to it that you're hired as one of Michelle's employees."

She rang the silver bell, but there was no need since Wilson had already returned. Devlin's beer bottle was perched on top of a silver tray along with a frosted glass and a small crystal bowl of pretzels.

Devlin's gaze bounced from the butler to Maude, then back again. "So, what did you have in mind?"

Maude chuckled, waving a hand in Wilson's direction. "Why, the solution is right in front of you. You'll be her butler!"

MICHELLE WORTHINGTON dodged a pair of teenagers gathering their book bags in preparation for walking out to the bus stop on the corner.

"Hurry it up. The driver won't stick around until you get there. Not after the charming vocabulary you were caught writing in the dust on his emergency door."

"Yeah, yeah," one boy answered, the half-dozen earrings he wore flashing and his oversize pants threatening to fall from his hips.

"And tighten your belt a notch, please."

Roscoe Bailey—or Rusty as he was known to his friends—tossed her a look of frustration, but did as he was told.

"Thank you." Turning, Michelle caught Samantha Brune settling onto the couch and slipping a romance novel from her pocket.

"Sammy, there's no time for that now. Wait until you're on the bus. Willie, Kirk, comb your hair! We can't have people thinking you don't own a mirror, can we?"

Michelle didn't know why she bothered. She'd learned long ago that for her kids—runaways and foster home "dropouts"—one of their last forms of control in life was dawdling on the way to school. Somehow, they had an innate sense of timing that allowed them to be close enough to catching the bus on schedule, but late enough to make it wait.

The doorbell rang, impatiently, stridently, causing Michelle to take the obstacle course of books, boom boxes, and gym bags at an even quicker pace.

"Annie, can you help get these kids in gear?" she shouted in the direction of the kitchen where one of the older teenagers was doling out sack lunches.

Not for the first time, Michelle damned the fact that Grace Coolidge, her second-in-command, would be gone for another month due to bunion surgery. Michelle was decidedly shorthanded—especially at times like these. But as she'd learned long ago, she would have to make do with what help she had. Since hers was a pilot program, there weren't many people who were willing to take a chance on a job that could disappear by the end of the year. Those that were looking for short-term arrangements usually couldn't stand the noise.

The bell rang again, and Michelle whipped open the door, offering a curt, "Yes! What do you want?"

Swiping a long, thick lock of hair from her eyes, she peered at the hazy outline of a figure who waited outside. Before the figure could speak, she mumbled, "Wait a minute, wait a minute," and fished her glasses out of her pocket.

Normally, she wouldn't be caught dead without her contacts, no makeup, wearing a seen-better-days pair of jeans and an oversize sweatshirt, but she'd just returned from the hospital where one of her charges had been having his stomach pumped after swallowing a stink bomb. Instead of greeting a deliveryman or some overzealous vacuum cleaner salesman, she should be getting the kids on their way to school so she could take a shower. A hot, melt-into-a-puddle-of-relaxation shower.

Sighing impatiently, she pushed the glasses onto her nose and the world swam into immediate focus. With it came a man. A formidable, lean, craggy-faced man, the likes of whom she had never seen here before.

"Yes?" she demanded impatiently, sure that this fellow with his close-cropped waves of wheat brown hair had to be at the wrong address. Otherwise, why would he be standing in the doorway of the Worthington Home for Teens with a duffel bag at his feet, aviator sunglasses shielding his eyes, and his frame encased in a dark suit, crisp shirt, and elegantly knotted tie?

But as the seconds flashed by, her stare grew even more fixed. A chill swept through her body, causing

Michelle to become rooted to the floor. The man on her doorstep looked like something out of a movie. With his conservative clothing and military-issue haircut, he was a perfect shoo-in for a member of the Secret Service. Or the FBI.

Dear heaven above, don't let him be from the FBI.

Half closing the door, she whispered over her shoulder, "Rusty, where exactly did you and Twink get that stink bomb?"

Rusty blinked at her in surprise. "I told you. It's left over from the package of stuff we bought for the Fourth of July. We got it at the corner stand by the grocery store."

"You're sure?"

"Sure I'm sure."

A sinking sensation gripped her stomach. If the government wasn't here about the out-of-season possession of fireworks, then which of her kids was in trouble now?

The door was pushed open from the other side and she pasted a benign grin on her lips, scrambling for some logical reason why she'd shut the panels in his face—especially when the stranger's features swam into view. So hard, so lean, so...intriguing.

"Michelle Worthington?"

As he called her by name, Michelle started, certain that the situation was even worse than she supposed. Maybe Twink had been doing more than playing with fireworks.

"Mmm?" She couldn't even manage a coherent reply. Not with so little sleep the night before and her body still buzzing from an onslaught of hospital coffee, adrenaline and a fresh injection of anxiety.

He held out a hand and she stared at it, realizing that he meant for her to shake it, meant for her to reach for him and allow her fingers to be swallowed in his clasp.

Michelle couldn't move, couldn't respond. It didn't matter that she'd been schooled in all modes of proper etiquette, that she'd been trained at some of the finest boarding schools in and out of the country. She couldn't bring herself to touch him. Not so purposely. So deliberately. Not when this craggily handsome man had come to arrest one of her kids.

Belatedly, she realized there had been enough of a hesitation on her part to appear rude. Even so, she couldn't move.

"Do I know you?" she asked instead, squinting at him—as if doing so might reassure her that he'd come for some innocuous reason and that was how he knew her name.

"No. The agency sent me."

"The *Agency?*" she echoed weakly. So he *was* from the FBI—or was it the CIA?

She must have paled because he was eyeing her in concern.

"I'm the butler to be named later."

The wry quirk of his lips brought her attention to the hard angle of his jaw, but Michelle's mind caught one word and held on to it with the intensity of a dog with a bone.

Butler.

Over a month ago, she'd begun making inquiries with several of the local agencies concerning hiring someone who could serve as a chauffeur, handyman and gardener at Worthington Home. When her advertisement for a male housekeeper had unwittingly resulted in her hiring a thief, a drunk and a transvestite, she'd opted for the term *butler* since it sounded far more sophisticated. Her only real stipulation for the job had been that the applicant be a *man* with experience in such duties.

With upward of a dozen young, wayward teens in foster care at the Worthington Home, Michelle had thought it would be in the kids' best interests to introduce them to a positive male role model. So many of these teenagers had come from broken homes, were runaways, or had been deserted by their parents, she'd thought a kind, grandfatherly gentleman would be just the thing to inspire some confidence in the masculine sex.

What she hadn't expected was a combination of Jeeves and the Terminator appearing on her doorstep.

"No." She didn't realize that she'd spoken aloud until the word burst from her lips. "Oh, no, this will never do."

The man removed his sunglasses, the entire motion so smooth, so graceful, it put her own earlier fumbling attempts to shame.

"I beg your pardon?"

Buried deep in his voice was a lilt, an intonation, a feathery, British inflection.

A *British* butler?

How traditional, how fascinating.

How awful.

"No, you won't do." She raked his form from head to foot again, even though she'd seen everything there was to see. "You won't do at all."

"Why?"

She opened her mouth to respond, hesitated, then stepped outside, closing the door behind her.

Unfortunately, the man on the stoop didn't counter her move, didn't even step aside, so she was forced to press up against him, her back to the heavy wooden planks, her thighs brushing his own firm legs.

"This..." she said slowly, as if explaining an elementary equation to a child, "is a place of refuge—a home, you might say—for teenagers in need of foster care. Many of them have been in trouble with the law." The last two words were whispered lest her charges realize she was speaking about them.

"Don't they know that?"

"Know what?"

"That they've been in trouble with the law."

She glared at him. "Of course they do."

"Then why are you whispering?"

She fought the urge to stamp her foot. What a disagreeable man. She was doing her best to let him go as easily as possible, with his dignity intact, and he didn't seem inclined to take the hint.

"I see no reason to blatantly advertise the fact."

"Even to me? Their butler?"

Before she could respond, he'd reached around her and opened the door. She was still scrambling for some sort of answer when he scooped up his duffel bag, brushed past her, and entered the hall.

"You can't go in there!" she gasped, running after him.

He dropped his luggage to the floor with a thud and tucked the earpiece of his sunglasses into the pocket of his suit jacket so that the spectacles hung there, drawing attention to his firm chest. Such a masculine chest.

Stop it!

"I'm afraid that the agency gave you the wrong idea," she tried again, taking a different tack. "I cannot—*cannot*—pay for your services without at least interviewing you first." There. The perfect statement to squelch this man's hasty assumptions.

"You won't be paying for my services at all."

This time, it was her turn to mumble, "I beg your pardon?"

"I've been sent here by an anonymous donor. My salary has already been paid in full for the next two months."

"Paid?" she echoed weakly.

"Yes." He withdrew a folded sheet of paper from the inside pocket of his suit jacket. "In addition to my services, I've been instructed to put the Rolls at your disposal."

"The . . . what?"

But she knew, and the anxiousness gathering in her chest increased. Taking a step, she drew aside one of the lace curtains situated on either side of the door. Parked in the driveway, next to the rattletrap van, was a gleaming vintage Rolls-Royce.

"No, no," she murmured more to herself than the gentleman waiting behind her. "This won't do. Not at all."

"Why?"

She spun around, glaring at him. "Can't you see? In this neighborhood, that thing will be stripped and vandalized in a matter of minutes."

"I don't think so."

The way the statement was uttered made her wonder if the car had some sort of antitheft device that would vaporize an assailant at twenty paces.

He held out the paper he'd taken from his pocket. "My references."

Michelle didn't want to take the sheet. She didn't want to feel the way the heat of his body would linger on the paper, but she really had no choice.

Taking it with two fingers, she scanned the list of names, addresses, and phone numbers, growing more and more concerned with each one she saw. Dignitaries, wealthy businessmen—even a member of the British aristocracy, for heaven's sake.

Her lips tightened and the alarm bells in her head began to ring. Daddy. This man had been sent by her father. She knew it.

"I also have experience as a medic."

"Oh, really?" she inquired briskly, her suspicions hardening.

"In addition, I've been asked to tell you, by this anonymous donor, that if you accept this gift, the donor may consider future investments in the Home."

"Oh?" She looked at him then, her eyes narrowing. He looked just like the sort her father would send her way. Tall, lean, successful, fairly reeking of the affluent life-style that Michelle had turned her back on years ago. Gerald Worthington had never accepted the fact that his daughter could not be as easily controlled as his own trade negotiations. He hadn't been able to fathom why she had felt an overpowering need to do something meaningful with her life, and he'd understood even less why she would want to spend her time with troubled teens. As far as he was concerned, there were government agencies available to handle that sort of thing and his daughter didn't need to dirty her hands in such affairs.

She folded her arms under her chest, then regretted the action when the stranger's gaze flicked in that direction. "What sorts of investments would this anonymous donor be offering?"

"Something in the form of a part-time tutoring center."

Trust her father to pick the one thing she and her kids needed the most. He'd probably had her under surveillance by a private investigator for weeks. A heat rose in her cheeks. He might even know about the way she'd rushed one of her kids to the emergency room little more than six hours ago. If so, it would be just like him to use such a fact to point out how unsuitable a "Worthington heir" was for such work.

She held the paper out to him. "Look, Mr...."

"Rhett. Devlin Rhett."

Her brows rose. Rhett the Butler. It was too incredible to believe.

"Mr. Rhett. I apologize for the inconvenience, but I have no need for my father's charity at this time."

"I wasn't sent here by your father, Miss Worthington."

And bears didn't romp in the woods.

"There is no need to lie for him."

"I was *not* sent here by your father."

His tone, his inflection, the intensity of his eyes nearly persuaded her to believe him. Nearly.

But even as she wanted to reject the offer out of hand, Butler Rhett had unknowingly struck her Achilles' heel. A tutoring center. How long had she dreamed of such a thing? Quite often, her charges were so behind in their studies that they needed personal, professional help. From time to time, Worthington House benefited from volunteers in the surrounding community, but it wasn't a service to be relied upon.

Even so, this man was wrong for this place. Completely and utterly wrong. He would frighten some of the more impressionable kids—and the teenage girls...

He would distract them. Worse yet, he might attract them.

But a tutoring center...

"I assure you, Miss Worthington, other than the fact that the donor wishes to remain anonymous, there are no strings attached."

"None other than hiring you."

His lips twitched. "Exactly."

"How do I know you are who you say you are?" she demanded.

His brows rose. "Why would I claim to be anything else?"

Why indeed? Nevertheless, he wouldn't be allowed within a mile of her kids until she'd had a chance to check him out.

Chapter Two

"Come with me, please."

To Michelle's infinite irritation, Mr. Rhett left his duffel bag in the hall where anyone could see it, anyone could inquire. But he did follow her. Not meekly, not docilely. No, he sauntered after her in a way that had the hairs on the back of her neck prickling as if he were studying her intently—as indeed he was, she realized when they passed a portrait mirror at the end of a crooked hall.

Their progress was followed by at least a half-dozen curious pairs of eyes, but that was nothing compared to the commotion that erupted when the door was opened and the car was discovered.

"Wow!"

"Look at that!"

Sighing, Michelle called, "Go to school—and make sure Willie is with you! He's in the backyard batting balls."

She thought she heard them complying, but Michelle guessed it was the Rolls and not her urgings that persuaded them to hustle outside.

Leading Mr. Rhett into her office, she shut out the noises, the chattering, the shouts to hurry, and quickly put a desk between them.

"Sit down." She pointed to one of the straight-backed antique chairs, but the man ignored her, crossing to look out the window instead.

"This is quite a setup you have here," he said, indicating the extensive gardens and the oval swimming pool surrounded by Greek columns and marble statuary.

Michelle cringed, sure he saw the untidiness, the overgrown yard, the untended outbuildings. But there hadn't been enough time or enough money to see to anything other than the house yet.

The muted slamming of doors informed her that the exodus for school had begun. Except for Twink—alias Pete Reynolds—who was still recovering from having his stomach pumped, and his twin sister Peg, who was on home study due to recurring anxiety attacks, Michelle would be alone for most of the day.

Unless she agreed to hire Butler Rhett.

"Somehow, this place seems a bit ornate for a youth home," the stranger continued.

Michelle didn't reply to his comment, didn't explain to this man why she'd converted this sprawling Art Deco mansion, which had once belonged to her grandmother, into a foster-care facility. It had been Nana's wish that the house be given to Michelle and put to some "useful purpose."

A shelter for teens in trouble may have been beyond what Nana had imagined, but after serving six months as a state social worker, Michelle had been driven to find a way to help, driven to find a way to keep these kids from falling through the cracks of the foster-care system. It was a pilot program that she hoped to see adopted throughout Connecticut. Here, those teens who didn't flourish in a setting with a more traditional family were brought together and encouraged to form their own unconventional ties with other kids and a pair of adult leaders. It was a method that was proving especially successful for teenagers who had already displayed a strong independent nature, since decisions here were made by the group rather than by the adults in charge.

Dragging her thoughts away from the harried activity occurring outside her door, Michelle stared at the man standing by the window. "Which agency sent you?"

"Freeds."

Spinning the Rolodex to the appropriate section, she punched the number into the telephone and waited as it rang on the other end—once, twice.

"Why would they send you without notifying me first?"

The man shrugged. "I suppose they thought you were desperate."

Desperate. Yes, she was desperate for help. This old house might be perfect for sheltering a dozen or more occupants, but its age caused a whole new set of problems. They had a leaky roof on the west end, a broken window on the second floor. Most of the faucets dripped and two toilets leaked. With Grace gone, there were countless phone calls Michelle needed someone to help answer, meals to serve, and a constant flow of visitors who had to be discouraged from coming at odd hours during the night. With two new teens scheduled to arrive in the next two weeks, she needed another employee.

She needed a cook.

She needed a handyman.

She needed a butler.

But she *did not* need this particular man. He was far too handsome—and she'd had her fill of handsome men. In her experience they were far too concerned with themselves, far too narrow-minded, far too... *handsome.* This one especially looked like the love-them-and-leave-them type, just as her ex-fiancé had been. He wouldn't remain at Worthington. He would want something more for his future. Something more in keeping with the references he'd shown her—and after her past problems with hiring for this position, Michelle was searching for someone with staying power.

The phone rang a sixth time, a seventh, and was finally answered.

"Freeds."

"Yes, this is Michelle Worthington. I need—"

"One minute please."

Michelle tapped her toe on the carpet in irritation. She hated being put on hold—almost as much as she hated being interrupted in midsentence.

"Michelle! Sam Freed here. Listen, I got an unusual response to your request for a handyman."

"Butler."

"Sure. Whatever. Anyway, I've got a man coming your way, excellent references—they all check out. What's more, there's a wealthy philanthropist who's willing to pay his usual salary for two months." He quoted an amount that made Michelle's mouth drop.

"You can't be serious."

"Yes, ma'am, I can. That's what one of those Limey butlers goes for these days—or half-Brit, anyway. He's got U.S. citizenship through his father, has lived here most of his life, so you don't have to worry about any alien work permits or anything."

"What if I decide not to use him?"

The silence on the other end was deafening.

"You're kidding, right? The man's F-R-E-E, free."

"He isn't acceptable for our needs."

"Why not? He can do the job, he has experience, he's a man. What more did you want?"

Before she could explain that she wanted someone ugly, someone settled, someone old—someone who wouldn't break her charges' hearts—Freed was speaking again.

"Your anonymous philanthropist has sweetened the pot with the suggestion of future donations, should you use this man."

"Why? Why is it so important to anyone whom I hire?"

She could all but hear the audible shrug in his voice when he answered, "Who knows and who cares? Take him and take the job he's offering to do. I gotta tell you, I haven't had another nibble for the position. Not at the salary you're proposing."

Michelle rubbed at the ache forming between her brows. "Fine. I'll get back with you when I've made a decision."

"Decision schmision," he drawled. "At least give the old boy a chance, hmm?"

Give the "old" boy a chance?

Samuel Freed had obviously not met Mr. Rhett.

DEVLIN TURNED HIS BACK to the window and propped his shoulders against the wall, wondering if Michelle Worthington knew how expressive her face could be. He saw each emotion march across her face. First the disbelief, then the stubborn denial, the resignation, the acceptance. Finally, she rubbed at a spot between her brows and briefly closed her eyes.

"Well? Will I be staying?"

She didn't immediately answer and he didn't push, realizing that she still had strong reservations about his being here.

Devlin couldn't blame her. After all, she was alone and in charge of a houseful of troubled teens. She should be wary of him—especially since her past hirings had been less than successful.

A grin tugged at the edges of his lips and he tamped it down, even as his mind fabricated an image of what she must have done when she'd found her latest butler trying on her high heels. Or at least that's what reportedly happened according to Maude's in-depth file.

When Michelle didn't move other than to rub at her temples, Devlin relented, deciding he'd give her a little more time to accept his presence in her house.

"Headache?" he asked.

"Mmm."

Her fingers moved to the back of her neck and he knew she must have one hell of a crick there. Although he hadn't let on, he knew exactly where she'd spent the previous evening—just as he knew every other move she'd made for the past forty-eight hours.

Idly, he wondered how she would feel if she knew the rest—his exact reasons for being here and her own proximity to danger. And what would she say if he confessed that it wasn't her father who had sent him, but her mother?

Until the moment he'd met her, Devlin had still been reluctant about agreeing to serve as Michelle's unknown bodyguard for the next two months—especially considering all these teenagers. Devlin had been uncomfortable with the idea of protecting someone without their knowledge of his true motives. But after meeting Michelle, he could see why Maude had insisted upon such measures. She was as fiercely independent and suspicious of help as her mother had warned him she would be.

Michelle had begun to arch her head from side to side in an attempt to relieve herself of the tension which must have gathered there, and Devlin finally took pity on her. Crossing behind the desk, he pushed her hands aside.

"Let me do that."

She started as if he'd touched her with ice-cold hands—which he had not. But as the rubbing increased, she wilted, then succumbed to the pressure, making him inexplicably aware of how she'd been strung as tight as a harp string.

"Have you done this before?" she murmured in a sleepy, don't-stop-what-you're-doing kind of voice.

"Massage?"

She summoned enough energy to shoot him a pithy look. He liked what it did to her eyes, the flash of fire it brought to the crystal blue depths.

"Butlering," she corrected.

"You saw my references. I'm an old hand at it." The lie came easily—as had the organization of a few people who would vouch for his skills at the job. But even as he reinforced his position as a practiced house servant, he felt a tweak of conscience—something Devlin wasn't accustomed to experiencing while working.

Devlin resolutely pushed the sensation away. After all, he'd been under Wilson's tutelage for some time now, and he thought he could pass as a fairly respectable footman.

With each arch of her head, Michelle's hair loosened from its barrette. Casting one last glance at the golden tresses tickling the backs of his hands, Devlin forced himself to remember why he was here and what he was supposed to be doing. He was her bodyguard. No more. No less. He would do his job, maintain his cover, and keep completely objective of the situation. Then, when the time came, he would leave. No ties. No regrets.

Devlin's gaze roamed the room with a practiced eye, taking in the woeful conditions of security in this place. The quick glance he'd had of the grounds had been just as disappointing. There was a fence around most of the property, but only an elf would have trouble scaling the divider.

"I was told that in addition to my responsibilities, you would be wanting me to install an alarm system," he said casually, paving the way for the improvements he would need to make as soon as possible.

She nodded, making him aware of the smooth, soft skin he encountered above the ribbed neckline of her sweatshirt.

"Mmm-hmm."

The relaxation techniques must have been working because she was growing sinuous, her voice adopting a sensual tone.

"We haven't had many problems with crime. Not really. But the home has been broken into once before—a kid thinking we had drugs in our infirmary. With the impressionable youngsters present at Worthington, I wouldn't like that to happen again. We've already bought the supplies for the system, but since we haven't had anyone who could install them, they're still downstairs in their original boxes."

"When did the break-in occur?"

He felt the shrug of her shoulders, one that made him aware of the fragility of her bone structure and the contrasting strength of the muscles encasing them.

"Six months ago."

"Six *months?*" His hands stilled and he stared at her bent head, realizing for the first time that Maude had probably been right when she'd insisted that Michelle was far too concerned with her work to realize what was going on around her. She needed protection. She needed guidance. She needed a keeper. And for now, it seemed he would be that man.

"Miss Worthington, I—"

From deep in the house there was a thud, a crash, then the unmistakable tinkling sound of shattering glass.

Devlin was instantly alert, but Michelle merely groaned. "Willie," she supplied succinctly. "He's intent on being the next Babe Ruth, and for some reason, all of his fly balls head straight for the kitchen window. I'll bet you a dollar he's hit it again."

She stood and Devlin was forced to take a step back.

"Michelle. Michelle!"

The cry came from the direction of the kitchen, growing louder as whoever was responsible hurried down the hall toward them.

Sighing, Michelle opened the door which she'd left ajar.

"Yes."

A freckle-faced kid—a *kid*—appeared, dressed in striped pajamas, his curly hair askew. "You've got to come quick! The kitchen window broke—it just disintegrated! Peg was washing dishes at the sink. She's cut real bad."

Devlin saw the way Michelle blanched, even as her expression remained calm. Immediately, he knew that there was more to her worry than the threat of a cut.

"Call an ambulance, Mr. Rhett. Now."

Michelle was relieved when Devlin didn't question the order, but he didn't immediately reach for the phone, either.

"Do you have a connection in the kitchen?" he asked, already loping down the hall.

Michelle hurried to keep up.

"Yes, but—"

"They'll want pertinent information. It would be better if we called from there."

Michelle hadn't thought of that when she'd made the instinctive order, but she was glad someone had shown such foresight.

Rhett tipped his chin at the boy and Michelle saw the way Pete's shoulders proudly drew back in his pajamas. "What's your name?"

"Pete, but they call me Twink."

"Pete, you go make the call," he ordered as they burst through the kitchen door.

As soon as Michelle saw Peg lying on the floor, blood spurting from a gash on her upper arm, she knew the scene was as dire as she'd supposed. The girl lay in a puddle of blood. Her face was ashen and beads of sweat were forming on her upper lip.

Devlin sank onto the tile as Michelle began talking to the teenager in an attempt to control Peg's obvious hyperventilation.

"I need some towels," Devlin said urgently, stripping his suit coat off and yanking at his tie.

Michelle tugged open a drawer and extended a stack of neatly folded dishcloths.

Devlin wrapped his tie around the folded squares as a makeshift pressure bandage. Then he took Michelle's hand, pulling her down to the floor beside him.

"Hold this to her as tightly as possible. She's going into shock."

"Hey, mister! I've got 911," Pete announced.

"Request an ambulance. Tell them we have a young girl—"

"She's fourteen," Michelle inserted.

Devlin nodded to Pete to relay the information.

"Pete, tell them she's going into shock and her breathing is labored."

"She suffers from anxiety attacks," Michelle clarified. "She's under medication and has an inhalator for when they occur."

Pete pointed to the familiar gray dispenser on the floor. "She took some, but I don't think it's helping."

"Pete, tell the operator all of that, too."

As the boy recited what he'd heard into the phone, Devlin said, "We need some blankets and pillows to elevate her legs."

"There's some in the closet to the left of the kitchen, just opposite the bathroom door."

Devlin nodded and jumped to his feet, returning seconds later. Just as quickly, he had Peg's legs raised and a quilt wrapped around her frail body.

"The ambulance is on its way," Pete said from his position at the phone.

"Great."

Devlin leaned closer to the girl on the floor. Her carrot red hair and freckles made her skin appear that much more ashen.

"What's her name?"

"Peg."

"Peg, I want you to look at me."

The girl's eyes fluttered, and she made a sound that was half mewl, half moan.

"Come on, Peg. Look at me."

At long last she complied, and Devlin smiled. It was a smile that tugged at Michelle's heart, full of cocky self-assurance and tender encouragement.

"Peg, I'm going to count to three. While I'm counting, I want you to slowly take a breath. Ready?"

Michelle watched in amazement as Peg focused on Devlin and struggled to breathe as ordered. Although her respiration continued to be labored, it did grow a little more controlled. Nevertheless, it was with palpable relief on all their parts when they heard the distant wail of the siren.

"Pete, go show them in," Michelle said quietly, not wanting to disturb the interaction occurring between Peg and Mr. Rhett.

The boy sped from the kitchen.

Within moments, the paramedics had rushed into the room and Michelle was pushed aside. After conferring with the hospital, one of the medics gave the girl a shot to sedate her and Michelle watched in relief as the color returned to Peg's cheeks. Only then did

Michelle realize that she'd been clenching her teeth so tightly her whole jaw ached.

Willing herself to relax, she turned her attention to Mr. Rhett. Despite her misgivings about hiring the man, she was glad he'd been here to help. There was something about him that instilled an immediate trust. He was calm, controlled, and seemed to have the emergency well in hand—far more than a mere butler should. It was as if he'd seen similar situations before and had known just what to do. In fact, if she was honest, he had been able to calm Peg much more quickly than Michelle had ever been able to do.

"We'll be taking her to Mount Holy Oak," one of the attendants announced as the gurney was locked into an upright position. "Which of you will be going with her?"

Devlin took an automatic step back, but Peg clung to his hand. "No, no! You have to stay with me."

Her speech was slurred from the sedative, and Michelle realized that Peg probably didn't even know what she was saying. Nevertheless, she felt a little pang in the region of her heart that one of her kids would turn to a stranger for comfort.

Devlin glanced at Michelle, but she waved him away. "Go on. I'll follow in the car."

As the gurney was being rolled to the doorway, Devlin reached into his trouser pocket and tossed a set of keys in Michelle's direction. She caught them merely on instinct.

"You can take the Rolls if you want."

She scowled, peering at the keys as if they were some sort of insect. "I don't think so, Mr. Rhett. We do have a van at our disposal."

He shrugged. "Whatever you say, Miss Worthington." Then he was striding from the kitchen and the swinging door was flapping into place.

"Who was that?" Pete asked as a strange silence slid into the room like an encroaching wave. Shifting, he lapped one foot over the other.

Too late, Michelle realized he was still in his bare feet and the floor was covered in glass.

"Here." She slid a chair toward him and watched him climb onto the seat. Although Pete was fourteen years old, he and his sister were both small for their ages, their slight bodies a legacy of being born premature, then being neglected for a dozen years.

"He thinks he's our new butler," Michelle said, unable to keep a shred of bitterness from feathering her tone.

Pete must have caught the disgruntled note because his brows lifted. Not for the first time, Michelle was convinced that he was some sort of wise old man masquerading in a boy's body. There was something far too penetrating about his gaze, and he saw much more of what was really happening in the world around him than many adults did.

"A butler, huh?"

Michelle nodded and reached beneath the sink for a dustpan, but her hands were noticeably shaky and Pete pointed to the chair opposite.

"I think you'd better sit down, Michelle," Pete said knowingly.

Michelle opened her mouth to protest, then realized she was feeling a little weak at the knees. She'd never handled the sight of blood well, and there was plenty of it smeared all over the tiles at her feet.

Deciding that good sense would have to take precedence over a show of courage, she made a detour to the refrigerator and withdrew a jug of milk. Then, reaching into the cupboard overhead, she removed a bottle of chocolate syrup.

She set them on the table and Pete's eyes widened in delight.

"Since neither of us drinks liquor, Pete, I think we could use another kind of bolstering." She retrieved two glasses and a spoon. "Why don't you pour?"

As she sank into a seat, Pete prepared the chocolate milk—mixing a concoction so dark and rich that the spoon could nearly stand by itself.

"Make sure you taste it first," Michelle warned. "You just had your stomach pumped, remember? It might not take too kindly to an injection of sugar."

But Pete had already gulped down half his glass and was smacking his lips. Chuckling, Michelle opened the cookie jar and pushed it in his direction. "Be my guest."

He took two and began to eat them with a voraciousness that belied the fact that he was more than well fed.

"Aren't you going to have any?" he asked between bites.

"I'm not really hungry," Michelle said, wishing her own rattled nerves could be soothed with milk and cookies. Out of politeness, she took a sip of the chocolate in her glass, but when her stomach threatened to revolt, she pushed it in Pete's direction. "Here. You finish it."

Pete eyed her as if she'd lost her mind in refusing the treat, but he didn't allow her time to reconsider.

"When will you go to the hospital?" he asked, a dark, sticky mustache lining his upper lip.

"Soon." What Michelle didn't say was that she was trying to regain her own equilibrium enough so that she dared to get behind the wheel of the van.

"That guy sure calmed Peg down."

"Yes. Yes, he did."

"I think he'll be a good butler."

Michelle hesitated, knowing that she should make it clear that Mr. Rhett hadn't been hired yet, but she exhaled instead. There would be time enough to explain all that after she'd collected Peg from the emergency room. In the meantime, Michelle wasn't about to voice her suspicions to a fourteen-year-old kid. Nor was she about to try to explain to him that her strongest objections to Mr. Rhett's employment lay in the fact that Peg had turned to *him* for comfort, and that she thought her father was responsible for sending him. Such reasons sounded childish even in her own head.

"I think it's a good sign that Peg was able to rely on someone else," Pete said thoughtfully, chewing on his third cookie.

Yes, but how would she feel if Mr. Rhett disappeared as quickly as he came? Michelle wondered.

"What's his name?"

"Mr. Rhett."

Pete grinned. "Rhett? Rhett the butler? Like in that movie you made us watch?"

Somehow, Michelle was sure she would be hearing that particular question quite a few more times in the next few hours.

Chapter Three

Feeling a little more in control, Michelle rose, reaching for the key ring hanging on the Peg-Board by the door. "I'll be back as soon as I can. Will you be all right or should I take you with me?"

Pete drew straight and proud. "I'll be fine on my own, Michelle."

She fought the smile that pulled at her lips.

"If you say so, but I'm still calling Miss Frieda next door to come look in on you. In the meantime, I want you to go upstairs and lie down—and stay away from the cookie jar," she said, pointing in the direction of the crumbs on the table. "I don't want to have that gut of yours pumped out again, understand?"

He laughed as if she'd told a hilarious joke, and she couldn't help chuckling herself. After all he'd been through, that kid must have a cast-iron stomach.

She was nearly out the door when Pete asked, "Will you be bringing the butler back with you?"

Michelle opened her mouth, paused, then said, "I don't know. I've got to think about it."

"Don't think too long. One good windstorm and our roof will be halfway to Kansas. That last butler guy never finished fixing it."

"Yeah, yeah," Michelle quipped, then frowned, realizing she'd unconsciously adopted one of Rusty's favorite responses.

She really did need another adult to talk to at Worthington House. But was Devlin Rhett the answer?

Or was he another problem?

MICHELLE ARRIVED at the hospital less than five minutes later feeling decidedly grubby and unkempt and wishing that she'd at least had the opportunity to change clothes and brush her hair since the last time she'd walked into the emergency room.

"Michelle, hon-ey!" a buxom woman from behind the registration desk greeted with a wide smile. "Long time, no see."

"Very funny, Ruth."

The nurse chuckled, her dreadlocks bouncing in delight. "Girl, we're gonna have to get you a group rate."

"I should say so," Michelle groused good-naturedly, slapping her insurance cards and guardian identification onto the Formica counter.

"Don't bother," Ruth said, pushing them back. "When I heard you were on your way in, I copied the information from Twink's chart."

"Thanks." Michelle stuffed them back into her purse. "How is she?"

"She'll be fine. They're stitching her up now."

Michelle's stomach rolled. For as many times as she'd been in this place with the injuries of one teenager or another, that was one procedure she couldn't handle. Stitches. One look at the needle threading through human flesh and she passed out.

Ruth chortled again. "You're looking a little green. Why don't you have a seat in the waiting area and grab a cup of coffee."

"Thanks, Ruth."

Castigating herself for being the coward she was, Michelle rounded the corner to the carpeted lounge, then stopped dead in her tracks when she saw Devlin standing with his back to the wall, staring her way.

"You."

The minute the word popped from her lips, Michelle could have kicked herself. She should have prepared something clever to say—or at least something intelligent. But no, she'd somehow thought that Devlin would still be with Peg and she'd have time to gather her wits about her.

"Peg's getting stitches."

"Yes. Ruth told me."

"Ruth?"

"The nurse at the desk."

The room fell silent and Michelle scrambled for something to say, anything that would help to reestablish the fact that she was the employer and he was the prospective employee.

"My father never told me about you," she said casually, sinking into one of the chairs.

"I am not here at the request of your father, Miss Worthington. I thought I made that clear before."

She sighed, knowing it had been foolish to attempt to trap him into revealing that Gerald Worthington was the anonymous donor. But she'd had to try.

"I appreciate everything you've done, Mr. Rhett," she began, straightening in her chair and wishing she'd remained standing. There was something about the way he towered over her, so intense, so elegant, so self-confident, that she felt all the more grubby and inadequate. Even if he hadn't been sent to her by Gerald Worthington, he may as well have been. In a scant hour, he'd undermined her own sense of accomplishment and made her feel like an adolescent struggling to gain the attention of her busy father.

"Mr. Rhett, I appreciate everything you've done today," she began again, trying not to look at the bloodstains on an otherwise perfectly starched shirt. Reluctantly, she darted a glance at his face, noting with surprise that his eyes were a rich cerulean blue— nearly turquoise—his jaw angular, and his mouth...

Fascinated, she watched as he slowly removed a sucker from between those lips and held it up for her inspection.

"Want one?" he asked.

The contradiction of such a suave man enjoying a lollipop was so disconcerting she could only stammer, "N-no, thank you, I—"

"I've got something in cherry as well."

Cherry. Her favorite flavor.

"No, I—" She cleared her throat, once again employing a stern facade and a pithy tone. "You must have been a very good boy for the doctors to have given you two."

The slow, potent grin that spread over his lips should have come with a warning label.

"The doctors didn't give them to me."

Her mouth made a round O.

"And I'm very rarely good."

The comment sent a rash of gooseflesh up her arms. She blamed the reaction on the stressful hours already spent at this hospital, but she feared the answer wasn't quite so simple.

She eyed him askance. "Do you mean to tell me you carry them with you?"

He nodded slowly, his gaze so intent that they should have been talking about something far less trivial than candy.

"I quit smoking."

"When?"

"Twelve years ago."

"I see." But her answer was weak. She was paying far too much attention to the way he was sliding the sucker back into his mouth.

"Did you bring the Rolls?" he inquired, his voice low and deep and smoky.

"No."

"Then you'd better give me your keys."

She bristled at the command. Wasn't *she* supposed to give the orders? "Why?"

"I've got the blankets we used on the way here. I thought I'd make a place for Peg to lie down for the trip home. They gave her some drugs for the anxiety so she's pretty well knocked out."

Michelle took a deep breath and sprang from her chair. "Mr. Rhett, I believe you're jumping the gun here. As much as I appreciate your help with this—" she said as she waved her hand vaguely "—situation, I haven't accepted you as an employee yet."

He didn't respond, and it irritated her that he thought her objection a moot point.

"Your keys." He held out a hand, palm up, and she was struck by the long fingers, blunt at the tips, and callused in a way that proclaimed he was no stranger to hard work. She had a flashing vision of this man answering the door at Worthington in his somber suit, then another more insistent image of him in jeans, stripped to the waist, pounding nails into the shingles of the roof.

Get ahold of yourself, Michelle, she inwardly chided, but it was impossible to subdue the flurry of excitement racing through her body.

She'd been around teenagers far too long—far, *far* too long. Perhaps if she'd spent more time with people her own age, accepted a date now and then, she wouldn't find herself attempting to confront a prospective employee while her knees trembled and threatened to dump her back into the chair.

"Mr. Rhett, I—"

He took the sucker out of his mouth, his features growing stern. "Look, Miss Worthington. I don't mean to rattle your chains or disrupt your schedule. I've been sent here to do my job, and I think you could use me. If you have a problem with the situation concerning who pays me, you'll need to take that up with the Foundation's board of directors and have them contact my employer. In the meantime, I have a job to do." Again, he held out his free hand. "Your keys."

She considered continuing their argument—considered it and abandoned it. This wasn't the time or the place to push her point, especially since her views were probably spurred by reasons that were more selfish than practical.

The realization was enough to prick her conscience. If this man *hadn't* been sent by her father to undermine her efforts and convince her to abandon such pursuits, she would be foolish to antagonize a prospective donor with the refusal of his gift.

But that didn't mean the matter was finished. Not at all. She wouldn't be satisfied with having this man serve as Worthington's butler until she knew everything about him, especially with regards to who had sent him here.

Digging into the pocket of her jeans, she retrieved the ring of keys. "Very well, Mr. Rhett."

His eyes narrowed, but she could not miss the gleam of satisfaction she saw in their depths.

"Does this mean you've agreed to accept my services?"

"For the time being," she said noncommittally. "But I think you should know that there is far more to this job than answering the door and installing a security system. You'll also be expected to plan meals, ferry teenagers to school activities, escort unwanted visitors from the premises and complete a host of household repairs."

"I do believe you're still trying to dissuade me, Miss Worthington."

"No, I'm trying to warn you. Judging by your credentials, I think you're in for a rude awakening. My teenagers have nothing in common with the types of people you've worked with before."

"You think so?" There was something about his tone that hinted at a secret knowledge on his part.

"I *know* so. They require a firm hand and an unconditional acceptance."

"I think I'm up to the challenge."

She opened her mouth to argue his claim, then decided against it. Let the man see for himself what was involved. Within a week, he would probably come to the same conclusion her father and her ex-fiancé had reached—that this was a dead-end job for a Worthington heir. They'd been so wrapped up in their high-powered, monetary world that they hadn't bothered to look beneath the surface of her work. They'd never discovered the plain and simple fact that there were lots of worthwhile things to be had in life that money couldn't buy.

Love.

Joy.

And the honest smile of a child.

THEY ALL RETURNED to Worthington Home little more than an hour after they'd left. When they did, an elderly woman was waiting for them by the back door.

Michelle fought the urge to sigh. As much as she appreciated Frieda Kleinschmidt and the way the woman was more than willing to help out on occasion, Michelle wasn't sure if she was up to all the questions the ninety-year-old matriarch would be asking. The woman was a born talker and rarely let an opportunity pass to inform whoever was in earshot just what she thought about everything from dental hygiene to Hollywood gossip.

"How is the girl?" Frieda asked anxiously as Devlin lifted Peg from the van.

Peg's arms circled laxly around his shoulders, but she was still groggy from the medication.

"She'll be fine, Frieda." Michelle handed her a bottle of pills. "Will you add these to her other medications in the kitchen cabinet?"

It was a less than subtle means to get the woman away from Devlin until Michelle had decided how to explain his presence, but the gambit didn't work.

"Sure, sure. Who's he?"

When she gazed curiously in Devlin's direction, Michelle was forced to make an introduction.

"Mr. Rhett, this is our neighbor, Frieda Kleinschmidt. Mr. Rhett is our new...butler," Michelle said, faltering on Devlin's official "title," which seemed so snooty.

Devlin nodded in the woman's direction, thinking the wizened old lady looked too frail to even hold herself upright. Her body was short and slight, her hair a puff of white cotton candy arranged into tight pin curls. But her eyes were a deep brown and twinkled with a rabid interest.

"I took a minute to remake Peg's bed upstairs, then cleaned up some of the mess. I'll show you where to go, Mr. Rhett." She turned to Michelle and shook a warning finger in her direction. "You'd better take a shower and a nap."

"Frieda, I—"

"Go." Frieda beamed. "Mr. Rhett and I can handle things until the children come home from school, can't we, Mr. Rhett?"

Her expression was full of sweetness and a shred of mischief that Devlin couldn't ignore.

"I don't see why not," he answered, willing Michelle to follow Frieda's suggestion so he could have a better opportunity to study the layout of the house.

It was clear that Michelle wanted to protest, but her weariness must have got the better of her, because she reluctantly acquiesced. "Very well. If you don't mind sitting with Peg."

Frieda waved away the comment. "Nonsense. Peg and I will watch some television together. I'd appreciate the company. Heaven only knows my own family doesn't visit often enough. Come along, Mr. Rhett."

Devlin followed the woman into the kitchen. In a glance, he saw that the blood had been mopped up and most of the glass swept into a pile. The arrival of the van must have interrupted Frieda in the middle of her task.

Frieda headed down the hall and made her way up an elegant, curved staircase which had probably seen many a grand entrance in its day.

"I don't mind telling you, Mr. Rhett, this old house holds a lot of fond memories for me."

"Oh, really?"

"Michelle's grandmother and I were quite the pair during our day. We used to run around the countryside like a pair of hooligans. I can't tell you the number of times we scaled that gnarled willow tree to get in and out after dark—especially before they remodeled the place. Even so, I know every inch of this house as if it were my own."

"It's very kind of you to come help this afternoon," Devlin said, at a loss for what to say. But he soon realized that Frieda didn't need any encouragement to keep talking.

"I was thrilled when I heard Michelle would be coming here to live after her grandmother's passing. Just thrilled. This ancient barn of a building needs some life in it, and those kids of hers are just the ones to do it."

She took a moment to gather her breath at the top of the staircase, then continued, "The girls' rooms are to the right, the boys' to the left. Michelle and her assistant take the two in the center."

"Her assistant?"

"Grace Coolidge. The woman's had foot surgery, poor thing. But I daresay she delayed the inevitable long enough. Those toes of hers were getting so twisted and swollen she couldn't wear anything but a pair of slippers," Frieda explained as she led the way, her rubber-soled orthopedic sneakers making soft squishing sounds against the polished hardwood floors.

"Here we are." She swept a door open to reveal a spacious area housing two twin beds, an old-fashioned armoire, and a pair of heavy bureaus.

"The far bedstead is Peggy's."

Devlin had already guessed as much since only one bed had the covers swept back in readiness.

He settled the girl onto the mattress and she made a sleepy sigh, then rolled to her uninjured side and snuggled into the pillows.

Frieda clucked in concern and began to pull the covers over the teenager's shoulders. "Poor lamb," she murmured. "I'll just show you your own bedroom, Mr. Rhett. Then, I'll come back and sit with her."

"Yes, ma'am."

At his reply, she straightened, peering at him intently, her hands on her hips.

"You don't look like a butler."

He didn't take the bait. "What is a butler supposed to look like?"

"I was always partial to Mr. French, myself," she said, referring to a television show that Devlin hadn't seen since he was a child. "In my opinion, you're a little too... athletic for such a highfalutin job."

"I try to keep fit."

"I'll just bet you do." There was a coyness to the remark that made him think it was meant as a double entendre—the last thing he would expect from a woman in support hose.

"Well." She sighed suddenly. "Come with me. 'All My Children' will be on in a few minutes, and since I've volunteered for invalid duty, I'll have a chance to see what all those rascally characters have been up to for the past week."

She marched from the room and Devlin followed.

"Do you watch soap operas, Mr. Rhett?"

"No, ma'am."

"You should. You really should. I've learned quite a lot from them, you know what I mean?"

Devlin murmured noncommittally, almost afraid to ask just what she'd "learned."

But Frieda didn't seem to need anything more than that as an answer. She made her way downstairs with a speed he was surprised to see in someone so apparently frail, then retraced much the same path he'd taken earlier that day to Michelle's office. He snatched his duffel bag from the hall as they passed. On the opposite side of the hall, she opened a small door. "This will be your bathroom." She leaned close as if imparting a secret. "They really should arrange something more private for you, but with all the teenagers in residence, it's first come, first serve as far as the facilities are concerned."

"That's fine."

The look she threw him was openly skeptical, as if she doubted that any "real" butler would agree to such indignities.

She strode to the next doorway, gesturing inside. "This is where they put the last man."

He glanced into the small chamber with its tester bed, oak wardrobe, and highboy. The quarters had a quaint, old-fashioned charm, despite the limited space.

"This will be great."

"Mmm-hmm," Frieda intoned doubtfully. "They haven't had an employee yet who really meant it when they said that. The last guy complained there wasn't room for his coordinating dress shoes."

Devlin choked on an involuntary chuckle, managing to disguise it by asking, "Beg pardon?"

She whispered, "He was a drag princess."

Devlin's brows rose. "A drag princess?"

"You know, one of those men who's light in the loafers and insists on dressing like a female."

Devlin didn't have the heart to explain that she had her royalty terms mixed up.

"I see."

"He kept sneaking into Grace's room and borrowing her Sunday-go-to-meeting dresses."

"How awful."

"Then he'd slip over to Michelle's and take her shoes." Frieda nudged him in the ribs. "You don't indulge in anything strange like that, do you?"

"No, ma'am."

"I didn't think so. But it doesn't hurt to ask." She sniffed. "Suffice it to say that Michelle's had quite a few men apply for the position of butler, but none of them have stayed.''

Devlin didn't speak, wanting the woman to tell him more.

''Of course the worst of them was that ex-fiancé of hers. He was the one to make all the legal arrangements for this place and proposition the state for the pilot program. But once all the political maneuvering was over and he was faced with actually living with the kids, he couldn't leave fast enough.''

''That's a shame,'' Devlin quipped, since it was apparent that Frieda was waiting for some sort of response.

''I'll say it is. He broke her heart, he did. Michelle's been awfully suspicious of men since then.''

''Even her father?''

Frieda made a sound that was half snort, half groan. ''She won't even talk about him. From what I was able to gather, he didn't have time for her when she was young, but now he's always interfering in her business. He doesn't like the fact that she's spurned the Worthington fortune and all that it entails.''

''Why? Surely, her father's money could come in handy at times.''

''Of course it would! But Gerald Worthington never gives anything away without a price. He told her once before that she was wasting her time here, that she didn't have what it took to make a success of it. He told her if she came here, she wouldn't get a cent of the family money until he died. Then, to add insult to injury, he offered to donate a quarter of a million dollars to the place if she agreed to serve as little more than a figurehead to the project. He even went so far as to say he'd take care of the hiring."

"She didn't go for it?"

"I'll say she didn't. The whole idea behind this program is that it be a group-run *home,* not some sort of institutional orphanage. All of the kids here have had trouble with their past experiences in foster care. The whole plan is to band these kids together and teach them that if they work together, they can succeed at anything they try. Her father would have turned the whole house into a minimum-security prison within a week, if you ask me."

Frieda's eyes narrowed, becoming uncomfortably direct.

"Just why have *you* come, Mr. Rhett?" But when he would have explained, she cut him off. "Don't answer that. It's none of my never mind why a man such as you has decided to come to this place. Just be warned..." Her expression grew fierce. "I wouldn't react kindly to anyone hurting Miss Worthington or one of her kids. If you remember that little fact, we'll get on fine."

Her chin jutted into the air, then she sniffed and turned on her toe, her rubber soles squeaking as she made her way back to Peg's bedside. As she retreated, Devlin found himself digesting the facts he'd been given. Although Maude's information had been more than complete, it hadn't been able to explain as much about Michelle's motivations for working at Worthington Home as the brief conversation with a concerned neighbor. For the first time, Devlin understood Michelle's preoccupation with her father's meddling, as well as her hesitance in dealing with another butler—a job which had probably been created when her fiancé had abandoned her.

She'd been engaged.

He wasn't sure why, but the information didn't sit well with him. Devlin chalked his reaction up to the fact that if the man returned for a visit, he could complicate matters even further, but there was more to it than that.

Sighing in impatience at his own line of thinking, Devlin dumped his duffel bag on the floor and stripped his jacket off, throwing it onto the bed. He needed a shower and a change of clothing, but first he wanted to get a better look at that window.

Chapter Four

Devlin waited, listening to the creak of the floor-boards as they marked Frieda's progress upstairs. When he finally heard the distant tinny noise of the television, he made his way to the kitchen. As he rolled his cuffs up, he inspected the pile of glass, then the broken windowpane.

But where was the ball? Michelle had immediately assumed that one of her teenagers had sent a baseball flying into the kitchen.

Retrieving the broom and dustpan, he swept the shards off the floor, and carried them outside to where he'd seen a row of garbage cans neatly situated next to the garage. After dumping the glass inside, he looked around him, but there was still no ball; not even a bat was in evidence. Surely, if Willie—whoever he was— had hit the ball through the window, he would have dropped the bat and hustled off to school.

A cool shiver of warning traced down Devlin's spine and he went back into the house. Crouching down, he peered beneath the table and the lip of the cabinets directly opposite the hole. When he caught sight of the broken fragment of a brick, his heart began to thump more methodically, and the instincts of caution he'd developed over years of security work slammed into place.

Glancing toward the door, he grew still, wondering where the boy Pete might be. But hearing nothing to indicate that there was anyone watching him, Devlin retrieved the brick, noting in an instant the scrap of paper taped to one side and the hastily scrawled message.

"Tell your father to back off!"

After examining the brick and the message, Devlin took a paper bag from a stack on the refrigerator and dropped the offensive object inside. He had friends on the local police force from his old army days. As soon as he could, he'd show them the note and see what they could make of it.

But even as the thought struck him, he doubted it would help. The paper was of the dime-store variety, as was the tape, and the message would be useless until Devlin could uncover some other sort of handwriting to use as a match.

Scooping the keys to the Rolls from the counter where Michelle had left them, he stowed the brick in the trunk, then surveyed the yard and house even more carefully than before.

He had a difficult task ahead of him in the next few hours. The property where Worthington Home was located was extensive, crowded with overgrown bushes and weeds, and dotted with a pool house, garage, toolshed, and storage shack. It would take some clever planning to get it all under surveillance with the mediocre cameras and equipment Michelle would expect him to use. Even so, Devlin wasn't as daunted as he might have been under normal circumstances. No, after witnessing the havoc the owner of the brick had already caused...

He was beginning to believe he'd come to Worthington Home in the nick of time.

BY THREE O'CLOCK that afternoon, Michelle was ready to tackle the world again.

Taking the steps at a brisk pace, she hurried downstairs just as the hall clock chimed the hour. She'd had a leisurely shower, a luxurious nap, combed her hair, put in her contacts and brushed her teeth. Of course, the fact that she'd dressed in a slim skirt and oversize sweater rather than her usual jeans could not be blamed on the presence of a new butler. Not at all. She'd merely felt like jazzing up her wardrobe a bit.

But the thought didn't ring true, not even to herself. Especially when she came to the bottom of the steps and found Devlin Rhett standing in the foyer. He was wearing a dark suit again, along with a fresh shirt and tie. But what she found hard to come to terms with was the fact that he was midway up a ladder cleaning the ornate picture rail.

In an instant, her gaze swept over the narrow entry hall, taking in the gleaming floor, the freshly polished brass, and the sweet odor of lemon wax and sunshine. Then her attention came zooming back to the figure on the ladder—a sight which jolted her anew.

For some reason, Mr. Rhett was an incongruous sight in the shadowy hallway. His powerful frame and angular features were much more suited to a boardroom or a power luncheon than to buffing her woodwork.

"Miss Worthington," he offered as a greeting, descending the ladder and standing to one side in a way that she knew was supposed to be a respectful form of attention, but instead caused her to study the muscles straining against the fabric of his trousers. "How are you feeling, Madam?"

Madam? Why did the word seem so unexpected coming from his lips?

"Fine, just fine," she murmured even as she shoved her fingers into the pockets of her skirt to hide the way they'd instinctively twitched at the mere sight of him.

"I took the liberty of beginning my duties."

Contrary to the way he'd behaved earlier, he was being very formal and staid. Despite that fact, every word he spoke had an uncanny ability to stroke against her nerve endings like a bare hand.

"I appreciate that. It looks wonderful."

"Thank you, Madam."

Madam. Once again, the word was jarring and so...so...unlike Mr. Devlin Rhett.

Her brows rose, but he must not have seen the reaction because he was folding the ladder and tucking it into the utility closet located beneath the stairs.

"I've noted that a good many of the sconces in the foyer are missing proper globes."

"Globes?" she repeated faintly, wondering what had happened while she'd been asleep to change the brash, take-charge, stubborn-headed man she'd met this morning into the epitome of the proper, British butler.

"Light globes," he clarified.

"Oh, yes," she said quickly, realizing her mind had begun to wander. "I'm afraid we haven't kept up with all of the bulbs that have burned out." She forced a light laugh. "We usually wait until the foyer is completely dark before replacing them."

He didn't respond to her joke. In fact, he was staring intently at her in a way that made her aware that his eyes were very, very blue.

"I'll see to the problem immediately."

I'll see to the problem immediately? He was sounding more and more British by the minute.

"Where are you from, Mr. Rhett?"

He didn't pretend to misunderstand her meaning. "Liverpool originally."

"Home of the Beatles?" she quipped.

Not so much as by a fraction of an inch did his expression lighten. "Quite."

"And you've been a butler for some time?"

"Off and on for over a dozen years. I received my education at the Chelsea Academy. They specialize in training some of the finest manservants. I have my credentials with me, should you need to see them."

Michelle hadn't known such specialized schooling existed, let alone that it supplied its graduates with "credentials."

"That won't be necessary."

"As you wish."

"Mr. Rhett..." she began slowly. "I'm sure that where you come from, such intense preparation is highly sought after, but here at Worthington, I'm afraid you're going to have to relax."

She wasn't sure, but she thought she saw a twinkle deep in his eyes.

"Beg pardon?"

Michelle couldn't put her finger on the exact reason why, but this man's sudden civility was making her increasingly nervous. It was almost as if he were playing a part on the stage and she'd misplaced her corresponding script.

"First of all," she began, pointing to his attire, "that suit has got to go. You look like you should be walking alongside the president's motorcade."

She thought she caught the briefest flicker of a smile, but when she peered more closely at him, she was sure she'd been mistaken. His jaw was just as hard as it had been moments before.

"What would you like me to wear?"

"Jeans would be fine."

"Isn't that a trifle casual?"

Trifle. What a wonderful word.

"Casual is best at Worthington, Mr. Rhett. This is supposed to be a relaxed and familiar residence, rather than some sort of institution. I wish my students to feel comfortable here."

"Yes, Madam."

"And another thing. Don't call me *Madam*. It makes me feel like I should be dressed in black and arranging the assignations of a dozen ladies of ill repute. You may call me Michelle or Miss Worthington, if you like."

A tingling began in the pit of her stomach and she wondered if he would choose to use her first name. She waited, her chest oddly growing tight.

But he only said, "Very well."

She heard a distant honk from the corner.

"That will be our gang." She glanced at the gleaming glass of the hall clock. "They're home from school."

She was already turning her back on him. It was safer that way. Far less nerve rattling. "I'll introduce you as they come in. Try to learn their names as quickly as possible."

"Very good."

Very good. Very well. His responses were still a bit more stilted than she would have liked, but she figured that an hour or two around her charges would loosen him up.

At the door, Michelle turned to tell him so, then closed it again when Devlin began to shrug out of his jacket and pull his tie free. He must have caught her gaping at him like a fish, because he jerked his head in the direction of his room.

"I'll just loosen up a bit before they get here, hmm?"

Michelle didn't offer a reply. She couldn't. Not when he was dislodging the buttons of his shirt to reveal a hard, tanned chest. Her mouth literally dropped open and her feet unwittingly trailed after him so that she rounded the corner of the hall in time to see him tugging the shirt completely off.

A jolt of pure sensation rushed through her body and she pressed a hand to the wall to steady herself when she nearly bumped into a small table which held the day's mail. Never before had she seen such wide shoulders taper into an incredibly narrow set of hips. Each ridge of muscle was so well-defined, she could have used his body for an anatomy demonstration.

Whoa!

Michelle whirled and leaned against the table, wondering what in the world had taken control of her senses. Granted, it had been some time since she'd been on a date, but she was not completely naive where men were concerned. She'd had her share of male companionship—she'd even been engaged, for heaven's sake!

But she could honestly say that she'd never met any man with a physique like that.

Even so, that did not mean that she should lose all sense of perspective, all sense of propriety, all—

"Ready?"

Somehow, he had emerged again without her hearing him.

Michelle cleared her throat, taking in his new attire. He still wore the pleated dress pants and shiny loafers, but he'd exchanged the rest of his ensemble for a creamy knit polo shirt. One that caressed his shoulders and—

Stop it! Just stop it!

Clearing her throat again, she gestured to the front door. "Shall we, Mr. Rhett?"

Michelle led the way to the front stoop and grasped the ornate iron railing, watching the troop of adolescents slogging the scant half block from the corner to the Worthington estate. Miraculously—or perhaps not so miraculously—as soon as they caught sight of the figure beside her, they quickened their pace, some even breaking into a run.

Beside her, she felt Devlin stiffen. Glancing his way, she was surprised at the way a muscle had begun to work in his jaw and she noticed that a bit of his tan had faded.

"Is anything wrong, Mr. Rhett?"

"No."

"You look a little—"

"I'm fine."

"Well, brace yourself. You're about to be sent through the gauntlet."

A herd of students was approaching, but Michelle stopped them before they could say a thing, holding up her hands for silence until they'd all crowded onto the lawn in front of her.

"Guys, this is a new employee at Worthington, Mr. Devlin Rhett. He'll be taking over the responsibilities that Mr. Perskin once had." Jack Perskin had been fired soon after Michelle had caught him trying on her new suede pumps.

"Mr. Rhett," she continued, "except for Twink, I mean, Pete, and Peg, whom you've already met, these are my guests."

She saw the infinitesimal lift of his brows at her word choice, but he didn't comment. Indeed, he looked as if he'd suddenly turned to granite.

Michelle pointed first to Roscoe Bailey. Since leaving this morning, his pants had slipped a notch again, but she didn't chide him for his attire.

"This is Rusty."

"Rusty," Devlin echoed, holding out his hand.

Rusty didn't shake it in the conventional manner, but linked his thumb with Devlin's.

"My man. Is that your car?"

Devlin shook his head. "No, but I've been told to offer it for your use."

"My *man!*" Rusty said with a little more enthusiasm, and Michelle rolled her eyes. The boy might dress and talk like a hoodlum from the streets, but deep inside, he was a puddle of Jell-O.

"Behind Rusty is Annie. She'll be graduating this year."

A tall, angular girl waved and dodged inside.

"Then there's Manuel."

A short, dark-haired, dark-eyed boy grinned up at him.

"Hi."

"And his best friend, Jason."

An intense sixteen-year-old teenager with Nordic features and a body already well past six feet tall, pushed past them both.

Michelle was sure that Devlin barely had time to register the fact that Jason's head was completely shaved, but for a Nike symbol.

"The girl with the pretty smile is Samantha."

The fifteen-year-old's mouth tipped in a sheepish grin and she tried to hide a bit more behind her book bag.

"Then there's Jessica, who loves to cook, and Marie, who doesn't."

The two giggled.

She pointed to the last pair of boys. "And these two are our budding sport stars, Willie and Kirk." Eyeing the wiry boy with spectacles, she said, "Willie, I want to speak to you about that window."

"Huh?"

She didn't give him time to protest. Turning, she held open the door, shooing her charges inside. "Get out of your school clothes and get changed for household jobs. You know the rules, so don't try to tell Mr. Rhett any differently. Chores, an hour of homework, then, if you pass inspection, the rest of the evening is yours unless you're on kitchen duty."

There was a host of grumbling, but the teenagers complied, used to the daily routine. As they filed past, Michelle added, "By next week, we'll have two more students in our care—Valerie Munns, an unwed mother-to-be, and Burt Escalson."

"Sounds like you've got a full house."

"Yes, and that's just the way we like it." She waited until all of the teenagers had made their way inside before saying, "If you'll wait a minute while they settle down, I'll show you around, Mr. Rhett."

DEVLIN WAS SURE he put her off guard when he stood obediently in the foyer while she shepherded her charges to their assigned study areas, plied them with milk and cookies, and listened to the highlights of their days. Then, after the house miraculously settled into a sedate murmur, he watched as she tiptoed back, gesturing to him with a crooked finger.

"This way, Mr. Rhett."

She climbed the staircase with utmost efficiency, one which made his attention drop to the sway of her hips as she took the treads. He liked her in that skirt. It suited her willowy frame and made her legs seem that much longer.

"We'll start up here, first. The girls' rooms are on the—"

"Frieda already explained all that to me," he interrupted. "Girls' rooms on the right, boys' on the left, you and Grace in the middle."

"You know about Grace?"

"Bunion surgery."

Her brows rose. "Evidently, Frieda was very thorough in her indoctrination."

He merely smiled, knowing she was dying to find out what else Frieda had told him.

Reluctantly, she continued, "The only real duties you'll have up here is ensuring that the linen closet is stocked. The kids are in charge of seeing to their own clothing as part of the training to help them fend for themselves once they leave here. The linens are usually Grace's responsibility, but I'm assigning them to you until she returns."

She arched a brow as if she expected him to argue, but he merely offered her a slow smile.

"That will be fine."

Michelle frowned and twisted the knob to a huge walk-in closet. "In addition to the linens, we keep emergency supplies here—candles, lanterns, a first aid kit.''

After he'd had a good look at the confines of the room, she closed the door, leading him across the hall. ''This bathroom has a leaky toilet and a dripping faucet. I'd like you to take care of them as soon as possible.''

''I'll do that.''

Again, she studied him, and he had the distinct impression that he wasn't behaving as she'd supposed he would—and quite suddenly, he knew what she was trying to do. She'd meant to overwhelm him with the list of repairs and odd jobs involved, things no respectable, professional butler would be expected to manage. Devlin certainly couldn't imagine Wilson doing half these tasks.

''Good. Well...'' She brushed past him again, leading the way farther down the hall. Wrenching open the last door, she pointed to a narrow set of stairs. ''This leads down to the kitchen, but we've had some problems with a few of the steps. They need to be reinforced.''

''I'll see to it right away.''

An expression flashed over her face, one that was nearly desperate in its appeal. ''I'm afraid that isn't all. There's the roof to fix, rain gutters to attach, the pool filter to repair, the garden to manage. Then there's the—''

He stepped close and she broke off, retreating until her shoulders were pressed against the wall.

"Miss Worthington," he said lowly, inching even nearer, so near that he caught the scent of the shampoo she'd used earlier. "If I didn't know better, I'd say that you were trying to scare me into leaving."

He planted his hand on the woodwork above her head, delighting in the way her whole body tensed at the action.

"I don't know what you mean," she offered quickly, but it was apparent to them both that she did.

"I'm not leaving," Devlin stated slowly.

"I didn't intimate that you should."

"Didn't you?"

He used his free hand to trace one of the creases between her brows. "Then what has you frowning in such utter concentration?"

Immediately, her face became blank and devoid of all worry, but it was apparent from the set of her shoulders that she wasn't as relaxed as she wished to appear.

"You still object to my being here, don't you?"

She didn't answer and he continued, "But it's obvious to me that you can use my help. In fact, it's obvious that you need an army of employees. So if it isn't the nature of my work that you object to, then you must take exception to me personally."

"Oh, no, I . . ."

Her voice trailed away into breathy silence and his finger slipped, stroking the length of her cheek.

"What do you have against me, Michelle?"

The use of her name caused her to start and he felt the telltale movement.

"Is it my background?"

"No."

But it was a bare whisper of an answer.

"Then is it my appearance?"

He wondered at the color which flooded her cheeks.

"Not at all."

"Then what, Michelle?"

She seemed to search for something to say.

"You're rather ... young."

"And that disturbs you?"

"Well, no, I merely—we *all* merely—expected someone older and more settled."

"Why?"

He continued to close the distance between them, unable to help himself. He was entranced by the way her breath caught in her throat and her eyes grew wide.

"Mr. Rhett, I don't think ..."

"What don't you think, Michelle?"

"I don't think that we should be standing ... so close."

But what had begun as a game had developed into something more. He found that he couldn't back away from her. Not yet. Not until events had reached their natural conclusion. What that conclusion would be, he wasn't quite sure. He only knew that the scent of her perfume and the guileless expression she wore was drawing him into a web of sensation that he hadn't expected from this job.

Then, before she could warn him against such an action, he erased the inches that separated them and placed his lips to hers.

The contact was immediate and electric, jolting him with its intensity. Before he was aware of what he was doing, he was leaning even closer, one of his arms sweeping around her waist to draw her against him.

She made a soft mewl of response, but did not resist. Instead, her hands curled into the fabric of his shirt and she lifted on tiptoe to meet him halfway. He felt her shift beneath his caress, her mouth opening to his.

His blood grew heated, rushing through his veins at a thunderous pace. Pulling her even tighter against him, he absorbed the way she fit into the contours of his body, her breasts flattening against his chest.

Just when he was ready to draw her into the darkness of the staircase, her hands became a wedge between them and she wrenched away, moving past him. A few feet away, she came to a stop, raking her fingers through her hair.

"What was that?"

The question was so soft and hesitant, he was sure that she hadn't meant for him to hear it, so he didn't answer. Bit by bit, he saw the steel ease back into her spine and knew that Miss Michelle Worthington, Woman In Charge, had returned.

"What was what?" he echoed, wanting her to know that he'd heard her, and, moreover, that he'd understood the instinctive question. What was the cause of that burst of passion? What was the reason for the inexplicable attraction humming between them?

Why them?

But Michelle chose to ignore him, continuing instead with her list of chores.

"You'll also need to do the shopping and the meals, Mr. Rhett. Since we usually eat dinner at six-thirty, I think that you should tend to the market and the food preparation first. We'll continue our tour later."

She began to march down the corridor as if nothing had happened between them.

Devlin found himself needing to stop her. He wanted to look at her, face-to-face, before she left. He needed to see her expression before she had the time to cloak it.

"How do you want me to pay for the purchases?"

Michelle paused, but didn't turn to face him—and he wondered exactly what she was trying to hide.

"We have an account at Mr. Quigley's Market on Rampart Street. A running list of supplies is kept on the refrigerator."

She took three more steps before he said, "It won't go away, Michelle."

He saw the way her hands balled into fists.

"What won't go away, Mr. Rhett?"

"That kiss."

"Perhaps not." She finally glared at him over her shoulder. She looked so proud, so stubborn, he was reminded of Maude's warnings of her independent nature. "But it must never happen again. Not while you're living under this roof."

But even as she strode away, he knew that such a wish was in vain. In the few scant seconds they'd spent in each other's arms, they'd opened a door which led beyond the realms of professionalism. The sensations they'd experienced would not be so easily pushed aside.

Chapter Five

When Devlin had agreed to this particular assignment, he'd thought it would prove to be a routine case. It wasn't the first time he'd been asked to protect a family member of a diplomat. True, he'd never infiltrated his client's normal routine under the guise of being a servant, but he'd still been sure that the task would prove routine. He'd even reassured himself that the presence of so many teenagers wasn't all that much to worry about.

But he'd been wrong. So wrong.

In the scant few hours since their return from school, Devlin had been blasted by a medley of rock and rap artists. He'd been given a crash course in the latest slang terms and had witnessed how a huge, tottering estate house could suddenly become very, very crowded.

Devlin supposed that part of the problem lay in the fact that he was new to Worthington. The residents found him an oddity. When he returned from the market with three dozen light bulbs and the makings for a quick meal, he was greeted by most of the "gang."

They were sitting on the back stoop, eyeing him in an overly suspicious manner. In an instant, Devlin knew he was considered an interloper here, although they didn't say anything outright. Even Rusty, who had extended an interest in the Rolls, was eyeing him closely.

"Where have you been?" Rusty asked, standing.

For some reason, Devlin had the impression that this was a test, and if he flunked it, the next few weeks would be a living hell. Vaguely, he wondered if Michelle knew how protective her students were of her.

"Miss Worthington sent me to the market. She said you usually ate around six o'clock."

"That's right," Manuel confirmed, taking his spot by Rusty. "So what'd you get t' eat, man?"

Devlin wasn't accustomed to being challenged by anyone, let alone someone so young, but he bit back his automatic response and held up the sacks he was carrying instead.

"Why don't you help me get these into the house and you'll see for yourself?"

It was apparent that the idea wasn't too popular, but Michelle must have indoctrinated them fully into sharing the responsibilities of the household duties, because several of them reluctantly accepted the groceries he extended, and the rest followed him to the Rolls.

"What does a car like this cost, anyway?" Kirk demanded as his arms were being loaded with bags.

"Too much," Devlin replied succinctly.

"Then why'd you bring it here?"

"It wasn't my choice. My employer told me to let you use it for the next few weeks."

Willie scowled at him. "I thought *we* were your employer."

Willie's response was telling, showing Devlin how these teenagers had been taught to handle most of the decision-making skills needed at Worthington.

"I was sent here on a trial basis," Devlin finally explained, not wanting to repeat the whole arrangement to this particular audience. "Miss Worthington will tell you everything tonight, I'm sure."

Before he could be questioned further, Kirk shouted, "Pizza! All right!"

At that pronouncement, Rusty's expression lightened. He slapped Devlin on the back, and for a moment, some of his distrust melted away. "My *man!*"

"Let's get all this inside," Devlin encouraged. "The sooner everything's been put away, the sooner we can eat."

The boys followed him into the house and hovered by the huge island worktable, watching his every move.

Deciding that he'd best assert what authority he had in the situation, he pointed to one of the bulging sacks.

"Put that away for me, will you, Rusty?"

Rusty studied him consideringly, then motioned for Willie and Kirk to join him.

Sensing that the others were just as curious about the "new man" and needed little more than a half-hearted reason to stay, he began assigning vegetables to be cut for the evening's salad, the table to be set, and garlic bread to be warmed.

Through it all, however, he became conscious of one boy who refused to participate. The bald one—Jason. There was something about him, something about the way he followed Devlin's every move, that caused Devlin to take stock of the teenager's arrogant posture and give-'em-hell attitude. He knew that it would take much more to win that boy's trust than giving him some carrots to dice or a spin in the Rolls.

So Devlin did his best to encourage the rest of the kids into helping him with the meal preparation. And when it came time to eat, he allowed them to load the bowls and plates and take them into the dining hall, so that he and Jason were alone.

"Do you like sports?" Devlin asked, gesturing to the Nike symbol that lay like a fuzzy check mark on the back of Jason's head.

Jason shrugged, his eyes remaining brittle and suspicious.

"What's you're favorite? Football? Basketball?"

Jason's hands delved deeper into his pockets. "I like both." The statement was an open challenge.

"Good. I'd enjoy tossing a ball around in the evenings or shooting some hoops."

"I don't need your charity, mister."

"I wasn't offering any. It's just a little hard to play one-on-one by myself. But..." he shrugged "...if you aren't any good, I can ask one of the other kids."

"I'm good," Jason asserted, then slammed his hand against the swinging door and strode from the room.

Sighing, and not really sure if that meant Jason would be playing with him or not, Devlin hefted a huge pitcher of ice water in each hand and made his way into the next room.

Once there, the noise was as deafening as it had been when the kids had come home from school. Remembering the crash course in butlering he'd been given, Devlin put one pitcher in the middle of the table and used the other to fill each of the glasses on the table. Then, he retreated to the far wall, planted his hands in the hollow of his back, and stared into space, waiting for further instructions.

But as soon as the occupants of Worthington Home were seated, they turned to look at him expectantly.

"Aren't you joining us, Mr. Rhett?" Michelle inquired.

He lifted a brow in obvious query.

"As I told you, we are very informal around here. You'll have to eat with everyone else if you want to be fed."

Michelle gestured to an empty seat at the end of the enormous table, and Devlin took his place, not noticing until that moment that he had been seated at the far end as if he were the patriarch of the group.

For some odd reason, the thought made him uncomfortable and he covered his reaction by staring in Michelle's direction, wondering if she was remembering their embrace. Judging by the pinkening of her cheeks, he'd wager he was right.

"Well, Mr. Rhett," Michelle stated, straightening ever so slightly in her seat. "Since you're new to our group, why don't you offer grace?"

"Offer Grace what?" he asked blankly.

The kids tittered.

"Pray, Mr. Rhett. Why don't you pray?"

He watched in astonishment as the teenagers joined hands. Following their lead, he took Pete's on one side and Willie's on the other.

"I'm not sure what you're accustomed to saying," Devlin finally said, when it became apparent that they were all waiting for him to continue. He didn't have the heart to inform them that he hadn't said a blessing on the food since he was five years old, and he wasn't sure if he could remember anything appropriate.

"Whatever you recite with your own family will be fine."

That didn't help him in the least. He was sure that Michelle wouldn't appreciate his own father's rote petition. Somehow "over the teeth, over the gums, look out stomach, here it comes" didn't seem at all appropriate.

"Mr. Rhett, everything is growing cold," Michelle reminded him sternly.

He cleared his throat, and as if on cue, every head bowed—thus increasing the pressure for him to perform.

"Lord, thanks for the food. Bless it. Amen."

There were a few titters around the table, but other than that, no one commented. Instead, they dove into the selection of victuals around them as if it were a race and the person in last place would be forced to starve.

"Don't wait to be served, Mr. Rhett. This group is used to fending for themselves at mealtimes."

He could bloody well see that, he thought as plates were circulated and helpings were dished out. His eyes widened when a piece of bread went whizzing by as it was thrown to Rusty on the opposite end.

"Willie!" Michelle chided.

"I'm following the rules," he grumbled.

"Rules?" Devlin asked.

Again, he thought he saw a hint of pink rising into Michelle's cheeks.

"As long as we keep one foot on the floor at all times and don't reach in front of anybody's face, we can get whatever we need," Willie explained. "I don't think that throwing the bread can count as breaking the rules, do you, Mr. Rhett?"

Devlin couldn't prevent the chuckle settling into his chest.

"No, Willie, I don't suppose anyone could fault you for that."

Devlin was sure that Michelle didn't appreciate his intervention in the running of things, but he didn't see any harm in his response. Especially when the other kids were laughing at the decision.

"I'll deal with *you* later, Mr. Rhett," Michelle muttered in mock threat.

But as the noise of the teenagers rose around them, their eyes met and clung.

Yes, Miss Worthington, Devlin thought to himself. *They would meet again later. Tonight. But he doubted that the mealtime rules would be at the head of their agenda.*

IT WAS DIFFICULT for Michelle to finish dinner with any show of normalcy—especially when her own taunting phrase rose up to haunt her.

I'll deal with you later, Mr. Rhett.

What on earth had possessed her to say such a thing? It was an out-and-out dare to a man like Devlin Rhett, she was sure. And she had played right into his hands. She'd all but intimated that she would be meeting with him sometime that night, when all she really wanted was to relax with her charges, then skulk up to her own room where she could be alone and gather her thoughts.

"Can I take your plate, Miss Michelle?"

She started, looking up to find Annie eyeing her in concern.

"Oh. Yes. Please do. I'm finished."

Annie continued to gaze at her long and hard, but she finally put Michelle's plate on the tray laden with crockery and backed into the kitchen.

Blinking, Michelle noted that she'd been abandoned to her own company in the dining hall. The meal had ended without her being aware of it, and the kids who were free from kitchen duty had left to amuse themselves for the evening.

Blast! She should have paid more attention to what was going on around her. As it was, her reaction would appear all the more telling to Mr. Rhett—and that was something she had to avoid. In her opinion, what had occurred between them in the upper hall had been a mistake, a momentary aberration brought on by two stressful days. She couldn't be blamed for leaning into the warmth of his body or seeking the comfort of his arms. Nor could she fault him for offering her his strength. But there would be no such future encounters.

There mustn't be any such future encounters.

She couldn't take the chance.

The last thought raced through her mind like a thunderbolt and she jumped to her feet, striding out of the room and making her way to her office. As she shut the door, she reassured herself that such assumptions were not only right, but necessary. She was the temporary guardian to a houseful of teenagers and it would be completely irresponsible for her to behave so foolishly in front of them.

Michelle's hands rose to her hot cheeks at the mere thought of what could have occurred had their embrace been witnessed by one of her kids. She didn't even want to think about such a possibility.

A knock sounded and she started.

"Yes?"

The door squeaked open and the subject of her thoughts appeared in the opening.

"Mr. Rhett," she breathed, wondering why she invariably sounded as if she needed a ventilator whenever he was around.

"You didn't eat much at dinner."

She did her best to appear unconcerned. "I wasn't very hungry."

"Liar."

She gasped at his quick, mocking retort, but bit back her own reply when she saw the tea tray he carried. It was laden with a pot of some delicious-smelling brew, a cup and saucer and a plate of tiny, crustless sandwiches. She was so surprised at the offering, that any sort of denial died in her throat.

"I thought maybe the pizza wasn't to your liking."

She did her best to appear stern. "We try to keep our meals as nutritious as possible here at Worthington, Mr. Rhett."

"I'm sure you do," was his easy response. He didn't appear in the least bit cowed. "But after I finished with the marketing, I doubted I'd have time to fix anything."

Michelle's eyes narrowed in sudden suspicion. "You do cook, don't you?"

He offered her a mocking smile. "Who doesn't, Miss Worthington?"

The answer told her nothing at all about his culinary prowess, but before she could question him further, he said, "One of my former employers has a fondness for British teatime and all it entails. She insisted I learn how to serve it properly."

He set the tray with its squat, simple teapot on the desk in front of her. With all the flourish he was employing, the crockery he'd assembled should have been fine china.

"I thought you might be the sort of person to appreciate such delicacies, too."

"And what 'sort of person' is that?"

"One with a fondness for details, a sense of history...." His eyes glowed in the dim light cast by the desk lamp. "Perhaps even a woman with a longing for romance."

Her lips tightened. "Mr. Rhett," she warned. "I thought I made it clear that there will be no more...hanky-panky between us."

His brows rose in obvious amusement at the archaic term.

"Hanky-panky?" he repeated. "I don't think I've heard that phrase used in ages." His tone dropped another notch. "Especially not in regards to necking in the hallway."

She gasped at his own blunt terminology. What they'd done couldn't possibly be labeled so crudely as *necking*.

Then again, she thought as gooseflesh scattered over her arms, maybe it could. But that didn't mean he needed to say such a thing out loud.

He was rounding the desk, ostensibly to pull the draperies shut at her window, but she thought there was more to the action than that. This man enjoyed putting her emotionally off-balance. For some reason, he got his jollies from making her react like a teenager instead of like a grown woman.

"What are you doing?" she gasped, when he leaned forward.

His smile was slow and all-knowing. "I'm retrieving the dirty juice glass on your desk."

"Oh." She damned herself for questioning him about such a simple thing, but she'd been so sure that he'd meant to touch her.

Her eyes met his, meeting the mischievousness and a smoldering warmth.

"I think it would be best if you left me alone, Mr. Rhett."

He didn't move. Although he now cradled the clear glassware in his palm, he didn't back away. Indeed, the heat of his body, his utter maleness, seemed to erase the distance between them.

"I don't think my leaving would help, do you?"

She ignored him, knowing that if she tried to respond to his bantering, her voice would emerge as little more than a croak.

"Come now, Miss Worthington. You don't really think that it will prove to be that easy to ignore what has happened between us, do you?"

Yes. It had to be that easy. She must *make* it that easy.

"I don't see why not," she said aloud.

"I never would have thought you were such a coward."

"There's a difference between cowardice and prudence, Mr. Rhett."

"I suppose you're right."

The silence thrummed between them with a tangible beat.

"Tell me, Mr. Rhett," she said, needing to reassert some sort of control over the situation. "Are you in the habit of flirting with your employers?"

His eyes darkened, sparking with a shred of self-deprecation. She watched avidly as the playful manner he'd displayed melted away and a will of iron took its place.

"Not at all. In fact, I can safely say I've never reacted to anyone this way."

The statement was enough to cause her stomach to tighten as if the ground had disappeared beneath her and she'd dropped a dozen stories. She hadn't been expecting such an honest answer. Nor had she expected how she would react to it.

"It's very unprofessional," he stated before she could regain her equilibrium.

Michelle wasn't sure how she was supposed to respond to that remark, so she remained silent.

"It's also very unlike me." The words were spoken slowly, as if he were absorbing their import as they passed over his lips. "But I've also been trained to heed my instincts, Miss Worthington."

Instincts. What did a kiss in a dark corner have to do with instincts?

Michelle didn't bother to ask. If the truth were known, she wasn't sure if she wanted to know. This conversation had already gone much further than was comfortable.

"Good night, Mr. Rhett," she said pointedly.

His ensuing smile was slow and rich, causing her knees to grow weak and her fingers to tremble. She was sure that he meant to ignore her none-too-subtle hint for him to leave. But to her infinite astonishment and regret, he stepped away.

"Very well, Miss Worthington. If that's the way you want it. I'll leave you alone with your thoughts."

When he left the room, she should have been relieved. Instead, Michelle sank into her chair and took a deep, shuddering breath, knowing she was doomed.

She'd never had all that much willpower. And in that instant, she knew for a fact she didn't have enough to ignore what Rhett the Butler did to her pulse every time he inhabited the same room.

DEVLIN WAITED until the house was quiet and still before taking the cellular phone from his duffel bag. Pushing one of the memory buttons, he tapped his fingers against the nightstand as the connection was completed.

"Ye-es?"

He grinned at Maude Worthington's theatrical drawl.

"I've been accepted as the butler to Worthington Home."

"Devlin, darling! I'm so glad she accepted your services. I was beginning to think my little girl had kicked you out on your ear."

"She tried."

"I'll just bet she did."

"She wasn't too thrilled about receiving a gift from an anonymous donor."

"Do you mean the car? Or your services?"

"Either. Both."

Maude chuckled. "I trained her right, didn't I? Never take candy from strangers—no matter what sort of pretty package it's in when it's delivered."

Devlin couldn't help harrumphing at the comparison.

"You don't think she suspects I'm behind it all, do you, dearest?"

"Not at all. She's sure her father is responsible."

"Ooo!" Maude cooed in genuine delight. "How delicious. That means he'll be on her S-list and I can still play the guardian angel."

"I wouldn't push things too far, Maude. Michelle's very shorthanded here. Her assistant is gone with bunion surgery and there are two more teenagers expected to arrive next week."

She made a clucking sound with her tongue, one he'd heard her do before when she was deep in thought. "Perhaps I should find a way to alleviate the situation."

Devlin sighed. "Don't you dare. If you tinker too much with the situation here, she'll probably fire us both."

"I'm her mother. She can't fire me," Maude replied with ultimate satisfaction.

"I wouldn't be too sure of that."

"Ahh, so you've had a taste of her temper." She giggled again. "Keep a stiff upper lip, Devlin, swee-tie. If there's anyone who can bend her stubborn will, I'm sure it's you. Meanwhile, enjoy yourself."

Devlin's brows rose at such an audacious com-ment. He wasn't here to enjoy himself. He was here to do a job.

"I'll call you at the end of the week, Maude."

"You just do that," she said.

But Devlin caught a gloating quality to her tone that he couldn't understand.

For some reason, it worried him no end.

Chapter Six

For the next few days, Devlin was kept busy accustoming himself to the routines at Worthington Home. Considering the way his first day had gone completely out of his control, he did his best to appear competent, formal and as invisible as possible. During the daylight hours, he studied the house, the floor plan and the electrical hookups he would need for the security system, and at night...

Well, at night, he did his best to decipher the creaks and groans he heard. It was the only way he could ignore the fact that Michelle Worthington had not lost her appeal.

Damn, he'd never known himself to be so intrigued by any female. He'd suffered through his share of attractions and affairs, but he couldn't remember a time when a woman only had to walk into a room to capture his attention.

By all rights, she shouldn't affect him this way. He'd certainly dated more flamboyant women—beauty queens, socialites and entertainers. But there was something about Michelle's cool, understated elegance. She had the undeniable wholesomeness of the ideal girl-next-door, combined with an unconscious sensuality that begged to be awakened. So far, Devlin had been able to resist and leave her at arm's length, but he felt his will weakening with each day that passed.

Disgusted with his own inability to focus on the job at hand, Devlin had set the alarm for five o'clock that morning. It was a technique developed from years in the armed forces, when he'd discovered that by continuing such a practice, he could get an amazing number of things done before most people bothered to rise. Today, he intended to run five miles, sweat this strange affliction from his body, then get on with the work at hand.

After sliding into a pair of gray sweatpants, he gathered his shaving gear and a change of clothing. Easing out of his room, he backed into the hall, ready for an invigorating shower, then a brisk jog around the perimeter of the property. Under the guise of exercising, he was sure he could develop a strategy for an outdoor surveillance system.

"Get out of there! It's my turn!"

The shout caused his head to lift and he turned to find a pair of teenagers banging on the bathroom door.

"Come on, Willie. It's picture day and we have to fix our hair."

Devlin considered ducking into his room again, but when two pairs of eyes turned his way, he didn't think there would be much point. He'd already been caught standing in the hall wearing little more than a pair of warm-up pants.

"Is anything wrong?" he asked, dumping his gear in the hall and quickly shrugging into a sweatshirt.

"Willie's in the bathroom and he won't come out," Sammy said, plunking her hands on her hips.

"I *can't* come out," came the distant plaintive call from the other side of the door.

Devlin motioned for the girls to stand back and leaned close to the panels. "What's wrong, Willie?"

"The doorknob broke."

"Just slip it back into the hole."

"I *can't*. It didn't slide out, it broke near the knob and there isn't anything to hold on to."

Devlin jiggled on his end of the knob, but to his consternation, the entire mechanism was jammed.

"Is it locked?"

"No."

"Are you sure?"

"Yes, I'm sure. Get me out of here!"

Devlin thought the boy's panic was a little more severe than the situation warranted, but when he twisted to find Annie and Samantha watching him, their faces set in scowls of disbelief, he changed his opinion.

"Hold on. I'll get some tools."

Making his way into the kitchen, he found Jason seated at the kitchen table eating toast and reading from a sports magazine.

"You're all up early," Devlin commented.

"Picture day," Jason explained succinctly, not bothering to look up. "The tools are under the sink."

Devlin didn't bother to ask how Jason had known what he'd needed. He supposed that the commotion in the hall had been loud enough for him to follow the progress of the emergency.

Retrieving the items he required, Devlin moved back into the corridor. By this time, they'd also attracted the attention of Pete and Kirk.

"Willie, is there anything inside that you can use as a makeshift hammer?"

There was a beat of silence, then, "No."

Devlin thought for a moment. The easiest way to get him out would be to take the door from the hinges, but the sliver of space between the wood and the floor wouldn't allow for much more than a screwdriver. If the hinges were as tight and squeaky as Devlin suspected, it would take a hammer to free them.

He turned to Annie. "Is there a window into the bathroom?"

"No."

Well, that blew the theory that there must be an easy way out of the situation.

"Willie, I'm going to pass a flat-headed screw-driver under the door. Grab it as soon as you see it."

"'Kay."

With each minute that passed, more of a crowd was gathering in the hall, until soon, judging by the prick-ling sensation at the base of his neck, Michelle Wor-thington joined them as well.

"What's going on?"

"Willie locked himself in the bathroom," Sammy supplied.

"I did not!" came his muffled protest.

Devlin finally allowed himself to look up at Mi-chelle, and doing so was like a punch to the gut. She was first-thing-in-the-morning clean, her hair still damp from her shower, her skin pink and soft.

"I need something he can use as a hammer, but it has to be small enough to slide under the door." Dev-lin was annoyed by the way his voice emerged more gruffly than he would have liked.

Her gaze raked quickly over his frame, taking in the casual sweat suit and running shoes, and Devlin found himself thanking heaven that he'd paused to drag on the top.

"I've got something."

She returned a few seconds later carrying her purse. After reaching inside the front pocket, she handed him a small, black *coup de bâton*—an undercover night-stick often used by police officers.

"Where'd you get this?" he asked, taking it, trying to ignore the warmth of her fingers as she passed it to him.

"I dated the son of the chief of police once."

He whistled under his breath, but slid the hard, tubular-shaped weapon under the door to Willie.

"Willie, at the top of each hinge, you'll see a ball-shaped cap."

"Yeah."

"I want you to slide the screwdriver between the lip of the pin and hinge, then tap it with the *coup de bâton* until the pin begins to separate from the hinge."

"Which one should I do first?"

"Try the bottom one."

There was a tapping on the other side, then the *ping* of the pin hitting the tile floor.

"Now do the others. You might have to stand on the edge of the tub to get the top one."

Devlin heard the pounding continue, a few grunts, and what sounded suspiciously like a curse. But at long last, there were two more telltale *pings*.

"Stand back," Devlin warned.

"Why?"

"Because he's going to kick the damn door in, that's why!" Sammy burst out.

All eyes turned in her direction and Michelle hitched a shoulder in the direction of the kitchen.

Before anyone could say anything, Sammy said, "I know, I know. A dollar for the cuss jar."

She stalked off and Devlin hid a grin. "Ready?"

"Ready."

Bit by bit, amid creaks and groans from the old door, Devlin pushed the panels out of their moorings, revealing Willie's wide smile. "Cool! I never knew a person could get through a locked door this way."

Devlin ruffled his hair. "Yeah, but it only works if you're already on the inside."

Willie laughed, but his merriment was cut short when Annie stamped her foot, saying, "Will you *get out?* It's picture day and I still have to curl my bangs."

Since the excitement was over, Devlin's audience melted away, leaving only Michelle.

"Very ingenious."

He shrugged. "I do what I have to do."

Her gaze was level and stern. "I just hope that I've seen the extent of your breaking-and-entering skills."

"Maybe. Maybe not."

She didn't seem to approve of his flippant reply.

"Mr. Rhett, I don't appreciate your levity."

"I take it you're not usually an early riser."

He saw the way her lips thinned.

"On the contrary. I'm always awake at this time."

She looked so prim, so proper, so completely ill at ease, that he couldn't resist baiting her. "Good. That will make adjusting our schedules around the teenagers that much easier in the future for some 'alone' time."

Michelle gasped, the color rushing to her cheeks so quickly, he couldn't resist laughing.

"You can't possibly...I don't think even *you* would have the audacity to...to insinuate that you and I...that we...would..."

She was sputtering like a fish out of water and he finally took pity on her.

"I just wanted to see how you'd react to the proposition."

Before she could vociferously deny any such arrangement, he placed a finger over her lips. "I don't have time to kiss you right now, Michelle. Nor do I have time to discuss this further. It's picture day."

Then, still chuckling at her openmouthed astonishment, he strode past her on his way to the kitchen.

MICHELLE MADE SURE that for the next few hours she was either barricaded in her office or surrounded by a half-dozen teenagers. She told herself that she was merely ensuring the professional distance that should exist between her butler and her, but as the morning progressed, she couldn't deny the little voice that informed her she was hiding.

But what else was she supposed to do? It wasn't proper for her to have...feelings concerning her butler. It was even less appropriate for her to be entertaining...urges.

Groaning softly to herself, she laid her head on the blotter, wishing that this whole situation would go away. This was the precise reason she hadn't wanted that man to stay here in the first place. This wouldn't have happened if Devlin had been sixty years old, or losing his teeth, or sporting a poor-quality toupee.

It was her own fault for not getting out more, Michelle supposed. When she and her fiancé had split, both Grace and Frieda had encouraged her to date as much as possible. Michelle had made an effort to respond to their matchmaking overtures a few times, but she'd soon abandoned the pretense. After all, even if she found someone whose company she enjoyed, her first priority was to Worthington—and there wasn't a man alive who was willing to saddle himself to this herd.

Nevertheless, if she'd been dating, if she'd been keeping company with nice young gentlemen, maybe she wouldn't be feeling so...so...needy.

Growling in impatience at her own insolence, she pushed that thought aside and lifted her head, reaching for the phone book so that she could call the glazier to check on the new windowpane she'd ordered at the beginning of the week. Willie had stridently claimed that he wasn't the one responsible for the broken glass, and with half a dozen witnesses volunteering their own testimonies, she knew she couldn't pin the blame on him. Even so, she couldn't understand how the kitchen window could have shattered all on its own.

Michelle had just confirmed that the pane was ready and had barely hung up the receiver when it rang again.

"Yes?" She automatically cradled the receiver to her ear with her shoulder as she reached for the books in front of her.

"Miss Worthington?"

"Yes."

"This is Principal Marks."

Michelle's eyes closed and she silently began to pray. Worthington Home had gone three weeks without any significant trouble.

"What's wrong now?"

Jan Marks chuckled softly on the other end. "Sammy left her picture money on the hall steps and she's beside herself worrying that she won't get her face in the yearbook."

Michelle sighed, knowing that she would have to retrieve the girl's book bag and take it to the high school herself.

"I'll be right over."

"Marvelous. That leads me to our second problem."

Second problem? Michelle's stomach dropped to her toes.

"Miss Gunderson, the home study teacher, has been having some problems with the starter on her car. The boys in the auto shop have promised to take a look at it, knock on wood, but I wondered if you could pick her up and take her back to Worthington for her session with Peggy this morning. I'll drop by this afternoon to ferry her to the next appointment.''

''Sure, sure. No sweat.''

''I'll see you shortly, then. Oh, and, Michelle?''

''Yes?''

''See if you can find Pete on your way here.''

Michelle groaned. ''He's skipping classes?''

''His advisory and first period teachers have both marked him absent.''

''I'll find him,'' Michelle promised firmly. ''You can count on it.''

Principal Marks chuckled. ''I was sure I could.''

Michelle sighed as she gingerly dropped the phone into the cradle, then stared at it as if to warn it against ringing. Standing and gathering her keys, she supposed that she was off for another typical day of chaos.

The thought was seconded when she strode into the hall, nearly colliding with Pete.

''What are you doing home?'' she demanded.

The boy immediately wilted against the wall, pressing a hand to his belly. ''I still feel sick,'' he said weakly. ''I think I'm having a relapse. I must have gone back to school too soon after having my stomach pumped.''

''Try that routine on someone who will believe you, Pete,'' Michelle said wryly. ''I saw the four bowls of cereal you ate this morning. You're the only person I know who eats them with orange juice instead of milk. Now go. You have five minutes to change out of your pajamas and gather your things. I expect to see written apologies to—"

"I know, I know. One for Principal Marks and each of the teachers I've missed."

"Exactly."

Sighing, Pete dragged his feet all the way to the staircase.

"Four minutes!" Michelle called.

His feet pounded up the treads.

Marching into the kitchen, Michelle grabbed her purse from the counter, ignoring the way her attention had settled onto Butler Rhett with the accuracy of a radar detector, even though she'd refused to look his way.

"Problems?"

"Sammy forgot her picture money and Pete is trying to use his invalid routine to cut class. To top it all off, the home study teacher needs a ride here. I've got to go to school and sort this all out."

"Do you want me to do it?" Devlin asked, drying his hands after loading the glassware into the dishwasher's top rack.

His question took Michelle aback. Although she supposed such errands fell into his territory, none of her other "butlers" had bothered to do much beyond their original instructions.

"No, but thanks." She couldn't avoid looking at him then, absorbing how broad and lean he looked in the form-clinging knit of his jogging suit. A tingling began deep in her belly and she prayed that this wasn't an example of what he intended to wear for the day. When she'd told him to relax his wardrobe, this wasn't exactly what she'd had in mind. If he spent the whole afternoon waltzing around Worthington, his buttocks well displayed, the muscles of his thighs emphasized, and the width of his shoulders enhanced . . .

She wouldn't be able to stand it.

She really wouldn't.

"Pete, come on!" she yelled, making for the door.

She had to get out of this place while she could still lay some claim to sanity.

DEVLIN WATCHED Michelle go, damning the fact that he would be unable to follow her without blowing his cover. But there was no helping the situation. Not when Peg was in the house and couldn't be left alone.

Hurrying to his own room, he slipped a small LED screen into his pocket after determining the homing device in the van was functioning properly. Then, he inserted a tiny hearing-aid-shaped receiver into his ear. The bug he'd inserted into the lining of Michelle's purse gave him a clear echo of the van's engine and the tinny music on the radio. Then, in the distance, he heard Michelle begin to lecture Pete on the dangers of being truant and he grinned.

Everything was working fine.

DEVLIN GLANCED at the schedule he'd outlined for himself the day before, then chucked the whole thing in the garbage can. He was swiftly beginning to realize that it was impossible to make a minute-by-minute "to do" list. Not in this house. Not with so many teenagers, so many interruptions and so much work to do.

He'd barely finished cleaning the kitchen and stacking the rest of the breakfast crockery in the dishwasher when Michelle returned. He heard the low murmur of her voice as she spoke to the woman who acted as the home study coordinator.

Walking into the dining hall which was serving as a makeshift schoolroom for Peg, he announced to Michelle that he would be downstairs investigating the alarm system Michelle had purchased a year ago.

"I'm not sure if I can hear the phone from there. Would you be able to answer it for a few minutes?"

"Sure, sure," Michelle assured him, not looking up from the notebooks scattered over the tabletop.

Devlin wanted her to glance at him, wanted to see what emotions she was entertaining, but she didn't budge. Sighing silently to himself, he supposed that it was one of her methods of putting him back into his place as an employee.

But then again, he thought as he waited a second more, maybe her reaction was much more complicated than that. Perhaps his presence disturbed her in some small degree. Enough that she didn't want to give anything away to the woman seated at the head of the table.

The thought was very intriguing. So much so, that it lightened his previously somber mood and added a jaunty bounce to his step.

Whistling under his breath, he made his way to the door in the kitchen that led to a dozen plank steps descending into a shadowy, ill-lit basement. The rough concrete walls had boxes neatly stacked against them, some of them labeled with names of the teenagers, so he presumed that even the kids were encouraged to use the storage facilities.

His whistle altered to a hum as he found the crates marked with the alarm equipment logo. Devlin recognized the name and the brand and shook his head. It was a good thing that he'd already begun to take some of his own measures to secure the house. Using the cellular in his room, he'd ordered small surveillance cameras for the front foyer, as well as the front and back doors. While repairing the roof, he would see about putting up some perimeter alarms and tying them all into the monitor which he'd placed in the armoire in his bedroom.

In the meantime, he would use the equipment Michelle had purchased to wire the windows on the upper and lower floors—although he was sure he would have to augment the supplies in the boxes with some of his own. Whoever had advised Michelle about purchasing this particular model hadn't taken a good look at the house, that was for sure.

Setting one of the boxes on the laundry table, he ripped the lid open, swearing when one of the copper staples raked across his knuckle and sliced into the skin.

"You'll have to put a dollar in the cuss jar for that particular word."

Devlin grew still, very still, listening to every squeak of the stairs as Michelle made her way into the basement.

"I thought you were helping Peg," he said, turning to face her and becoming very aware of the fact that they were alone in a darkened cellar.

"She's with her tutor. The woman comes from the junior high school once a week, gives Peg her assignments, and tries to offer her some personal help."

"It must be tough for Peg to keep up with the other kids in her classes with only one day's worth of instruction."

"I help her as much as I can, but that's one of the reasons a tutoring clinic would be so valuable."

Michelle took the last step and asked herself for the hundredth time why she was here and why she seemed destined to play with fire.

When Peg had begun to review her algebra, it had become apparent that Michelle was no longer needed and she'd wandered into the corridor, intent on the book work which was awaiting her attention.

But she'd never reached the door of her own inner sanctum. She'd never even made it halfway down the hall. Instead, she'd found herself dragged to the steps leading to the basement.

A part of her accepted the fact that she was inexplicably pulled to this man—even as it warned her that such an attraction would prove dangerous. But the other part...

The other part dared her to give him a taste of his own medicine, to unsettle him in much the same manner he'd disturbed her for the past few days. Even though he hadn't touched her since that first night, she knew he wanted to—and what was worse, she'd longed for him to do so.

And now, standing so close to him in the basement, knowing that it was her will, not his, which had brought her here, she knew that touching him would be inevitable.

Michelle looked down and saw a thin trickle of blood oozing from his finger.

"What happened?"

"Nothing. I grazed it opening one of these boxes."

"It looks like more than a graze to me."

She took his wrist and an instant awareness thrummed through her body, making her realize that this time, she had been the one to initiate the contact.

The stillness of the basement sifted around them, cool, tense and electric with its power. Michelle told herself this particular incident was different. This time, she was the one responsible for the heady sensation.

But even as she insisted such a thing to herself, she knew it wasn't true. There was something about this man. They only had to share the same room before a series of chain reactions began. Awareness. Attraction.

Desire.

The moment the word popped into her brain, she tried to banish it. But it was impossible to ignore the truth.

Looking up, she found him watching her, his own eyes darkening to the color of a stormy sea.

"What are you going to do, Michelle?" he murmured, and the velvet-on-steel timbre of his had the ability to send a flurry of excitement through her veins.

She stroked the knuckle above the wound, then took a clean handkerchief from her pocket and wrapped it around his finger. "You need a proper bandage on that."

It wasn't the answer he'd sought, just as the question he'd uttered had nothing to do with his finger. Not really.

"I thought you didn't want me to touch you again," he murmured. "What makes you think I'd be willing to give you such liberties?"

Her eyes closed for a fraction of a second. She remembered saying such a thing, but she'd known that abstinence was impossible—just as she'd known she was destined to kiss him at least one more time. Just once.

"Maybe you're right," she whispered. "Maybe I should leave you to your own devices."

But when she would have torn herself away from his side, he caught her around the waist, pulling her irretrievably against him.

"I don't know what's happening here, Michelle."

He didn't need to elaborate, she knew what he meant. Neither of them had anticipated the attraction that was pulling them together. But neither of them had the will to stop it.

"I want you to know that I've always been the kind of person who deals strictly with the job."

As he spoke, he drew her closer and closer.

"I've never mixed business with pleasure."

"I know that."

"But in your case, I can't seem to remember my priorities."

Then his lips were closing over hers and she was reaching on tiptoe to wrap her arms around his neck.

Chapter Seven

Devlin was like no man Michelle had ever known before. When she was in his arms, he had the ability to make her feel fragile and feminine, yet at the same time powerful and free. Her fingers splayed wide, testing the muscles of his back and shoulders, exploring the planes that she had studied surreptitiously for far too long.

Had it really only been a week since she'd known him? No, less than a week. Yet, she felt as if he'd been a part of her life for much longer than that. It had been such a relief to have him take part of the burden of Worthington Home. Often, when she went to perform a task, it was already done. But even the emotions generated by such niceties were nothing like what she was experiencing now.

Passion had never been like this for Michelle, not even with her fiancé. Oh, she'd tasted desire, she'd felt the rush of blood and adrenaline, but that was nothing compared to the overwhelming heat she experienced in Devlin's arms. He had the ability to cause her senses to rage. That was why she had tried to avoid him, just as that was the reason why she found herself here today, in a dark basement, in the midst of his embrace.

She ran her hands over his shoulders and down his spine, wanting to absorb his body into her own, wanting to know each nuance, each texture, each plane and valley.

Michelle made a guttural, mewling sound deep in her throat and he instinctively responded, his own arms sweeping around her waist, his broad hands cupping her buttocks and lifting her to him, pressing her against his arousal. The breath left her body in a whoosh and she strained even closer, knowing that her behavior was far from the calm unflappable woman she presented to the world. But until this moment, she hadn't known how hungry she'd been, how lonely. For this. *This*.

Their kiss became starved, fierce, their tongues twining in an intimate dance. Michelle felt Devlin shifting to carry her, pressing her back against the rough wall, but she barely registered the cooler temperature of the concrete. She could think of little else but the man who held her.

''No!''

Without warning, Devlin wrenched away, tipping his head back to gulp air into his lungs.

Michelle blinked, so stunned by his withdrawal that she could do little more than brace herself against the concrete and struggle to catch her own breath.

"What's wrong?" she finally managed to ask. But even as the words escaped from her lips, she knew. She knew it the instant reality rushed around them, reminding them both of who they were. Employer and employee.

But what about man and woman? Didn't that count for anything? a little voice whispered, but Michelle pushed it away.

Devlin had been right to stop things. It had been irresponsible of her to even approach him alone in the basement. After all, she hadn't come down here for any particular reason.

She'd come for this, for his embrace.

Again, she shoved the tiny murmur of her conscience aside.

Straightening, she tried to pull the mantle of leadership back around her shoulders. This lapse in judgment never should have happened, but since it had—at her own urging—it was up to her to set things right again.

"I'm sorry, Mr. Rhett. I'm afraid that I was the one to break our promise."

"Promise?" Even in the dim light, his eyes burned with an inner fire. "What promise was that?"

She shifted, wishing that he wouldn't make her spell it out to him. He knew just what she meant, but he wanted to punish her somehow. He wanted her to say the words.

"Our promise that we would never..." she waved her hand in an expansive gesture to indicate what had happened between them "...again."

This time, it was Devlin who straightened, Devlin who took control. "I never promised I wouldn't touch you...or kiss you."

The words were blunt, echoing in the room around them.

Knowing that she had to leave, now, before they crossed beyond the boundaries of mere passion, she tried to brush past him, but he caught her elbow, holding her still.

"Do you know what you've done to me, Michelle?"

His voice feathered over her skin, satin and iron, silky and hard.

She could only shake her head.

"I've always been a slave to duty. *Always*. I've taken great pride in the fact that I do my job and do it well. I've never allowed personal biases or sentiment to cloud my judgment or get in the way of what has to be done. Then, when I've finished, I collect my pay and leave."

She winced at the blunt assertion, wondering if he meant to do the same in this case. Collect his pay and leave.

Devlin tugged her irresistibly closer until her arm was pressing into his chest. He leaned close to murmur, "I've never had a woman get under my skin so quickly or completely."

The words caused her to shiver in delight and trepidation and she stared up at him, unblinking, wondering if the statement had been as hard for him to make as she believed.

"I don't want to like you, Michelle. I don't want to be attracted to you. Those sorts of feelings only get in the way."

"Of what?" The query was hard to push out of the sudden dryness of her throat.

"Of clear thinking and professionalism."

She didn't know how she was supposed to respond to that, so she kept silent.

"The thing that amazes me is that I would have never believed myself capable of being attracted to someone like you."

She stiffened as if he'd slapped her, but he held her firm.

"You're everything I've steered away from. Someone with roots, commitment, subtle beauty, an enviable strength."

The breath locked in her throat at the openness of his speech.

"You're dangerous, Michelle. Especially to a man like me."

"A man like you?" she prompted, hoping that he would tell her more, but he shook his head, releasing her and stepping away.

"You'd better go," he said instead.

"Why?"

"Because if you don't, I don't think I could keep from dragging you to that old pile of blankets in the corner."

He didn't need to say any more. An image of the two of them twined together in a passionate embrace, naked, dappled in sweat, was enough to spur her into walking to the stairs.

It mustn't happen. Not here. Not where she was supposed to be the bastion of respectability. It was her job to provide a good example for her kids, to teach them that there were times for restraint and abstinence.

Now was the best example possible.

"I appreciate your honesty, Mr. Rhett," she said as she took the first step.

"I still want you, Michelle."

His comment came out of the blue, knocking the strength from her knees so that she was forced to cling to the railing.

"So I think it would be best for all concerned if we kept our distance."

She opened her mouth, hoping to make some off-handed comment to disarm the potentially volatile situation, but she was infused with a slow anger. How dare he tell her what they should do? How dare he dictate to her the best way to handle her own emotions? Especially when she had asked him the same thing not a week before.

Turning, she stepped back onto the basement floor. Approaching him slowly, deliberately, she smoothed a hand over her forehead, then her hair, in a casual gesture that should have been completely innocent.

Should have been, but was not. Not when she forced him to look at her, to follow the line of her arm to where her breasts pushed against her sweater.

"I've never been very good at taking orders, Mr. Rhett."

A shimmering expectancy returned to the room, filling the air with its electric heat.

"Anyone who knows me is aware that I'm stubborn to a fault and very, very headstrong." She was so close to him now that she doubted a piece of paper could have slipped between them. "Therefore, I think you should be forewarned that if I stay away, it's because *I* choose to do so." She placed her hands on his chest and rose on tiptoe. "Understand?"

One palm slid behind his head to bring him down for her kiss. As before, the passion between them was instantaneous, bursting into life like a wildfire.

"Michelle?"

From some distant place, Michelle heard Peg's voice and she knew she had to step away from Devlin. But even as common sense demanded some sort of response, her body was not so quick to comply. As she took a step back, her lips lingered, as did her arms, until finally, there was enough space between them for her to breathe.

"Good afternoon, Mr. Rhett."

She turned then, sauntering with a model's grace to the staircase, knowing full well that his gaze had centered on the swell of her hips.

"Michelle, are you down there?"

Peg's voice was closer now and the upper door cracked open to reveal the fourteen-year-old girl.

It took a real effort to force away the languid pleasure which had infused her body, but Michelle did her best to appear quite normal. "Yes, Peg. What do you need?" Belatedly, she noted that her voice sounded far too thin and breathless even to her own ears.

"Principal Marks is here."

"Fine. Show her—"

"No, you don't understand. She's brought Kirk with her. He's been expelled."

Michelle was instantly alert. Running up the steps, she dashed into the foyer just in time to see Kirk being led inside by Principal Marks. His clothing was torn and bloodied, his hair disheveled, his face cut and bruised.

Michelle groaned. Kirk had already been suspended once for fighting with the local bully. Evidently, he'd been at it again. After all that had already happened today, what more could go wrong?

"Darlings! I'm here to help!"

Michelle froze, slowly looking beyond Kirk and the principal as the door burst open to frame a lithe, flamboyant woman dressed completely in pink from the top of her velvet turban to the tips of her satin shoes.

"Mother?"

"Yes, dear."

Maude was already tugging at her pink kid gloves.

Vaguely, Michelle heard Devlin approaching. As he walked past her, she felt a corresponding response in the region of her heart. Things had just become a hundred times more complicated between them.

Maude extended her gloves to Devlin, then handed him her pink makeup case. "I called earlier to see how you were doing. I assume that it was this delightful gentleman—" she patted him on the cheek as if he were twelve years old "—who informed me that Grace had gone under the knife." She shuddered delicately, then beamed at them both. "Aren't you going to introduce me to this marvelous crowd, dear?"

Michelle flushed, realizing that she'd hesitated long enough in performing such a duty to appear either rude or secretive.

"Mother, this is my...*our* new butler, Mr. Devlin Rhett."

"A *butler,*" Maude exclaimed in delight. "You're becoming quite progressive. I'm thrilled."

Michelle gestured to the other pair. "This is Principal Marks and one of my kids, Kirk Haines."

Maude blew a kiss in the general direction of the boy. "Hello there. I've heard so much about all of you boys and girls."

Kirk struggled in Principal Marks's grasp as if he were a puppy and Maude a dogcatcher. Finally, he managed to free himself and dodge into the kitchen.

At that moment, Wilson stepped into the hall carrying an armload of suitcases and hatboxes.

"Thank you, Wilson. Put those in Grace's room, will you? It's the one at the head of the stairs."

"Moth-er," Michelle protested.

Maude ignored her, sweeping her arms wide. "I rearranged my calendar, and, other than a few fittings, I'm at your disposal."

"For what?"

"Whatever you want me to do. I've come to help."

Michelle stared at her in disbelief. "What were you thinking of doing?"

"Well, I won't know until you tell me, will I?"

"Mother, I really think it would be best if you—"

"Don't bother to thank me any more, little one. What's family for if they can't help one another in a pinch, hmm?"

After kissing Michelle somewhere in the neighborhood of her left cheek, Maude swept up the staircase calling, "Wilson! Make sure you hang that Armani dinner gown up right away. I don't want it wrinkled."

Michelle waited until Maude was out of earshot before saying, "Only my mother would bring Armani to wear at a youth home." She rubbed at the ache that was beginning to gather right between her eyes.

"Is she serious about helping?" Devlin murmured.

"Unfortunately, I'm sure she is," Michelle said, her voice ringing with dread.

"Is that a bad thing?" Jan Marks asked.

"It's a very bad thing. My mother can't cook, has never cleaned. I doubt she even knows which end of a vacuum cleaner is up."

"What about... Wilson, is it?" Jan queried.

"He'll stay too, I'm sure. The two of them come as a pair." She took a deep sustaining breath. "Will this day never end?" she murmured.

Principal Marks chuckled and patted her on the arm. "Doubt it. You know what they say about bad luck coming in threes."

Then she went in search of the home study coordinator, leaving Michelle and Rhett alone again. But after a few seconds of tension-fraught silence, it was Devlin who excused himself.

"I'll just go check on your mother."

"Thank you."

Michelle waited until he'd disappeared upstairs, then sighed and went in search of Kirk to demand an explanation. *Bad luck comes in threes,* she thought as she pushed open the swinging door.

If that was the case, by her count, she'd had enough to last the week.

"WHAT ARE YOU DOING here?" Devlin demanded, slamming the door behind him.

Maude whirled, but Wilson didn't pause from unpacking.

"Sweetie!"

"Don't you 'sweetie' me. I want to know why you're here at Worthington."

She grinned, perching on the end of the bed. "I thought you'd be thrilled. This way, you can watch over the both of us at the same time."

"You said you could take care of yourself."

"I said I would leave New York for a few weeks. I put Puppy-kins in the kennel and—" she grinned, holding her diamond-studded hands wide "—here I am!"

Devlin growled, his hands balling into tight fists. "You've made things very difficult, Maude."

"How?"

He didn't answer immediately. He couldn't. Under normal circumstances, it wouldn't have mattered a bit if he'd been given two people to protect instead of one. But things were not normal here. In fact, they were quite out of the ordinary. He was faced with one client who had all the subtlety of a neon pink sign and another who didn't know his true reason for being here. Added to that was the fact that he was struggling to maintain a clear head and some manner of professionalism.

"Is something wrong, Devlin, darling?"

He glared at her.

"I promise I won't give you away."

He pointed to Wilson. "What about him?"

"Wilson won't tell anybody either, will you, Wilson?"

The old man blinked at them both.

"I didn't mean that I thought Wilson would blow my cover, I meant that this house can't have two butlers—especially when all my supposed training will be shown up by a professional."

Maude frowned. "I hadn't thought of that." She tapped a pink nail against her lips, then grinned. "I've got it! We'll say that Wilson is on vacation."

Wilson appeared suddenly perplexed and she quickly patted his hand. "Now, Wilson, I didn't mean I'd be sending you off somewhere. I just meant you could relax a bit, take in some sun, read a book. You can do that, can't you?"

"Yes, Madam." The reply emerged as a near question.

Turning, Devlin stormed to the door.

"You aren't angry with me, are you, Devlin?" Maude called.

He turned to find Maude genuinely distressed and he sighed. "No. You're fine. You're bloody well fine."

Then he marched into the hall, slamming the door behind him.

THE HOUSE WAS DARK and quiet, its inhabitants sleeping, before Devlin dared to make his way into the foyer again. He set up the ladder beneath the chandelier in the vestibule and set a bag of bulbs on the top rung, then removed from his pocket a surveillance camera no bigger than a penny.

Under the guise of checking the wire connections, he quickly hooked the lens to the upper bracket, then began screwing bulbs into the sockets.

"What are you doing?"

Devlin nearly dropped the sack. Twisting, he tried to keep his balance on the ladder even as he confronted a pair of bright eyes staring at him from between the posts of the railing. The thatch of bright red hair gave the boy's identity away.

"Hello there, Pete."

For the most part, Devlin had done his best to avoid any real contact with the teenagers at Worthington. He ate his meals with them, fixed their lunches for school, washed their linens, but he hadn't bothered to talk to them any more than necessary.

Tonight, it seemed his self-imposed reticence was being challenged.

The boy's eyes twinkled in delight at being called by his real name instead of Twink.

"Hello there to you too, Mr. Rhett."

"You can call me Devlin if you want."

"Really?"

"Sure."

Pete grinned, looping his arms through the banister and clasping his fingers.

"Whatcha doin'?"

Devlin gestured to the chandelier over his head. "I need to replace the light bulbs."

"Most of them don't work."

"I found that out my first day on the job."

Devlin returned to his task, screwing the last three bulbs into place. When he finished, he jiggled the sack filled with worn-out globes. "Too bad these aren't recyclable."

Pete nodded with utmost seriousness. "We'd make a fortune if they were." Then, after glancing over each shoulder as if he were being observed, he crept down to the ground floor and settled on the lowest step.

Sensing that the boy wanted some company, Devlin climbed down and put the ladder away under Pete's careful scrutiny. Then, he sat on the tread beside him.

"How's your sister doing?"

"Fine. She says her arm hurts now and then, but Michelle promised her a trip to the bookstore when the stitches come out, so Peg's being brave."

"She likes books?"

"Yeah. That's something Michelle insists on if you come live here. You have to read thirty minutes a day. She says it will make us smart."

"She's right."

"She says it's the smart people who can choose what they want out of life instead of having it chosen for them."

"That sounds like good advice." Devlin reached into his pocket, withdrawing a pair of suckers. "Grape or tutti-frutti?"

"What's tutti-frutti?"

"I have no idea, but it tastes good."

Pete grinned and chose that particular lollipop. After unwrapping it, he put the cellophane in the paper sack Devlin held his way. Devlin followed the same process with his own sucker.

"Do you like it here, Pete?"

"Sure. It's lots better than where I was before."

"Where was that?"

He shrugged. "A place in Westmont, about forty miles east."

"Did Peg like it in Westmont?"

"She didn't live there. We've only lived together once since the courts put us into foster care."

"That's too bad."

Pete's face screwed into a scowl. "It stunk. I promised to take care of her and they wouldn't even let me go to the same school. That's why I kept running away."

Devlin absorbed that statement, supposing that such a habit was probably responsible for Pete being considered a "troubled teen."

"How many times did you run away?"

"Sixteen."

Devlin whistled under his breath. "That's a lot."

"Yep."

"So, when did you come to live here?"

"About two months ago. Miss Worthington came to juvie hall to see me."

"Why were you in juvenile detention?"

"I stole some stuff to eat."

"Ahh."

"She came right up to me, shook her head, and said, 'You're a mess, Pete Reynolds, you know that, don't you?'" The boy laughed as if he'd given the punch line to a joke. "She was the first person in that place to talk to me like a real person instead of looking down her nose at me."

"What did she say after that?"

"She told me she could tell I was smart just by looking at my record—too smart for a regular foster home. So she asked if I wanted to be one of her kids."

"And you accepted."

"Only once she promised to take Peg, too." He took the sucker from his mouth and pointed it in Devlin's direction. "Michelle keeps her promises. That's why she has such a good reputation at juvie."

"They know about her there?"

"Of course. Everybody wants to be one of her kids. She knows you've been in trouble, but she trusts you, you know what I mean?"

Devlin nodded as if he understood perfectly—which he guessed he did, in a way. He'd seen Michelle interact with her kids and knew that she regarded them as equals with mutual problems to solve, not "street thugs" as many adults might regard them.

"That doesn't mean she won't come down on you like a ton of bricks if you get in trouble," Pete continued knowingly.

"She's a taskmaster, huh?"

Pete frowned. "A what?"

"She'll punish you if you deserve it, but she's fair."

"Yeah, that's it. She never hits you or anything."

The statement tugged at Devlin's heart since it bespoke of an experience of such treatment from other people in charge of his welfare.

A silence settled around them, but not an uncomfortable one. Realizing that there were times to talk and times to remain quiet, Devlin stared unseeingly at a point yards away, just as Pete did, sucking on the end of his lollipop. The two of them remained that way for some time. Then Devlin heard the way Pete lost his patience with the sucker, bit down, and began chewing on the chocolate Tootsie Roll middle.

Devlin laughed, remembering what it was like to be a kid filled with impatience when everything he wanted seemed just out of his grasp. But then he sobered. Not much had changed since becoming an adult. There were still things he longed to have, and they were still beyond his reach.

Such as Miss Worthington. Taskmaster.

Grasping the sack, he held it out for Pete's stick, then stood—all beneath the watchful eye of the kid they called Twink.

"Well," Devlin asked, taking his position by the light switch. "What do you think? Will all the sockets work?"

Pete shrugged. "We've never changed every single bulb before, so I couldn't say. That light's pretty old."

Devlin's hand dropped. "Do you want to do the honors?"

"Sure!" Pete grinned and jumped up, his bare feet making little sound on the wooden floor as he ran to the switch. "Ready?" he asked.

"Ready."

His stubby finger pushed at the switch and the vestibule was immediately flooded with light. Pete gasped, staring up at the sparkling crystal chandelier, then down at the miniature rainbows being cast onto the floor. "Wow," he breathed.

"It's something, isn't it?"

"Pete? Pete, why aren't you in bed?"

The distant call came from the second floor and Pete jumped.

"Gotta go," he whispered, rushing to the staircase.

"Hey, Pete," Devlin said when the boy was halfway up. When the redhead paused and turned, he asked, "What in the world possessed you to swallow a stink bomb?"

Pete shrugged as if the answer were obvious. "Rusty said he'd pay me a dollar if I could do it." He grinned. "Now he owes me a buck!"

As the teenager disappeared into the boys' wing, Devlin smiled softly to himself. For the first time since coming to Worthington, he'd found himself quite comfortable in the presence of a teenager.

Maybe they weren't all aliens, he thought, extinguishing the chandelier and making his way to his own room to check out the picture being broadcast by the surveillance camera.

Chapter Eight

Sunlight was pouring through her office window when Michelle heard the familiar voice call, "Val and Burt are here!"

Rising from her desk, she took a moment to glance in the mirror to ensure that her hair was smoothly clipped behind her head, her white shirt tucked neatly into her jeans.

Today heralded the arrival of two new charges, Valerie Munns and Burt Escalson, and as was the custom, the inhabitants of Worthington had organized a welcoming committee.

Michelle had always felt that first impressions were important, especially to the teenagers who came here. They were often accustomed to being shuttled from foster home to foster home, and they had become leery of the routine. Because of that, the kids who lived here felt it was important to make a ceremony of the day. A huge banner with Valerie's and Burt's names had been fastened to the front gate, yellow ribbons had been tied to a pair of trees near the front walk, and a special meal had been prepared.

As usual, Michelle brought up the foot of the gang as they rushed to the state-owned station wagon pulling to a halt near the front stoop. Unfortunately, as she took her place in the foyer, she noted that such a position brought her parallel to Devlin Rhett.

Although days had passed since their encounter in the basement, the memory of those long, overpowering minutes spent together hovered in the air between them.

Michelle was sure that Devlin's own thoughts echoed hers. She could see the evidence in the way the blue of his eyes had deepened and the line of his mouth had grown taut around the edges.

"After you, Miss Worthington," he said, holding the door wide.

Brushing past him, she couldn't ignore the warmth of his body or the subtle hint of cologne that clung to his skin.

She'd awakened early that morning, early enough to see him loping out of the house and jogging the circumference of the property over and over again for nearly an hour. By the time he'd finished, his body had gleamed with a sheen of perspiration and she'd wondered what it would be like to touch him just then—all sleek and hot and wet.

Stop it!

"It's a beautiful day, isn't it?" he asked as they took their places at the railing surrounding the front stoop. The kids were huddled around the station wagon in the driveway below, waiting for the first car door to crack.

"Yes, it is. Thank you."

The banalities seemed out of place between them, especially considering the fact that Michelle didn't want to exchange trivial chitchat. When Devlin spoke, it made it that much harder to ignore him, that much harder to fix her mind on something else.

"I saw you."

Devlin's statement was so low, she nearly didn't catch it.

"Beg pardon?"

"I saw you watching me. You really should take the time to draw your blinds early in the morning."

Michelle froze, flooded with embarrassment. He'd caught her gawking at him as if she were some teenager afflicted with a burst of hormones.

When he observed the way she'd grown still, her hands clenching the railing so that her knuckles grew white, he chuckled. "Feel free to look all you want, Michelle. Just remember...you promised not to touch."

Her face was hot as he made his way to the car, standing just outside the knot of excited kids as they welcomed a tall, skinny boy, and a girl who was obviously in the last few weeks of pregnancy.

Sammy turned to gesture for Michelle to approach, and she forced her fingers to relax enough so that she could let go of the supports, but it didn't stop the pounding litany that filled her head.

You promised not to touch. You promised not to touch.

Damn that man. She'd done her best to maintain a cool facade in his presence. She'd been calm, collected, and serene. So what right did he have to scatter her cool as easily as a cat scattered a flock of birds?

Straightening her shoulders, she marched down the stairs to meet the social worker who was rounding the hood of the car.

"Hi, Michelle. How are you this morning?"

Betsy Todd had worked off and on with Worthington since its inception, and Michelle was relieved to see that the plump, matronly woman didn't seem aware of the tension still gripping Michelle's muscles.

"I'm fine, thanks."

"Here're the files you requested." Betsy handed her a pair of thick manila envelopes. "If you need anything else, I'll see what I can do. We're still trying to find an interpreter for Valerie. So far, all I've been able to round up is some part-time volunteer help."

Valerie was completely deaf, a fact which had earned her a place at Worthington even though she had only recently been placed in foster care.

"I'll see what I can do on my end before..."

Michelle's words trailed off as she happened to glance up and see that Devlin was conversing with Valerie. In sign language.

Catching the direction of her gaze, Betsy grinned. "Well, well, well. I can see that you've already taken care of matters. That's a load off my mind."

Michelle didn't bother to correct Betsy's assumption that Devlin had been hired as an interpreter. Numbly she watched as Betsy supervised the unloading of luggage from the station wagon. She even managed a jaunty wave as the car pulled out of the driveway. But when the kids began to crowd back into the house, she caught her butler by the arm.

"Where did you learn to sign?" she whispered as the group passed.

He shrugged. "My kid brother was deaf. That's why my parents moved to the States. They thought he would have a better opportunity with his education here."

A perfectly logical explanation for such an incredible coincidence.

But as he entered the house, her eyes narrowed. She was beginning to believe this man was a little too perfect for the position of Worthington's butler. It was as if he'd been hand chosen for the position by someone with enough clout to force him to work at a place like this.

Someone like her father.

MICHELLE SPENT the rest of the afternoon ensuring that the two new occupants of Worthington Home were made comfortable. Burt was put in a room with Manuel and Annie took Valerie under her arm.

But she was soon to realize she wasn't the only person to help with the transition. By lunchtime, Devlin had taken all of the teenagers on "spins" around the block in the Rolls, Maude had plied them all with her special punch concoction—minus the usual rum—and the house was alive with noise and music and laughter. Even Wilson had helped ensure that new posters had been hung on the walls, new snapshots tacked to bulletin boards, and two new sets of dress shoes had been polished.

That evening, in celebration of the newcomers' arrival, a pool party was held—an event that was given an especially festive air when Maude took charge of the barbecue. Even Mrs. Kleinschmidt had come for the evening. She and Wilson had soon donned their brightest beach attire and were competing for the honor of the gathering's whitest legs.

Through the splashing, squealing and shouting of the teenagers, Devlin circulated with trays of drinks and hamburgers. Michelle's eyes followed him, not so much with interest this time as with anxiety and suspicion. Who had sent him here?

Who?

She'd tried to put a call through to her father with no success. He was involved in negotiations.

He was *always* involved in negotiations.

As an adolescent, Michelle had grown so sick of that particular phrase, she had stopped trying to communicate with the man.

Failing to reach him, she'd put a call in to Richard Lipton, the head of the trustees who handled funding for Worthington. Although he confessed that he knew the identity of her mysterious donor, he had refused to divulge the person's name. So Michelle had come full circle to the fact that Devlin Rhett was still far too perfect for the job as butler, and his being here was still fishy as hell.

"Would you care for a soda?"

She stared at the man of her thoughts, studying him with what she hoped were fresh eyes.

"Who sent you here, Devlin?"

"Your mother thought you needed a drink."

She ignored the way he'd misinterpreted her question.

"Who sent you to Worthington?" she clarified.

"So we're back to that, are we?"

She waited in silence.

"What has you so prickly and tense, Michelle?"

"I think it's a little too convenient that you know how to sign just when we need that particular skill."

He shrugged. "It's a coincidence."

"Is it?" When he didn't answer, she demanded again, "Who sent you?"

"You know I can't answer that."

"Then at least tell me why you're here."

A stillness settled around them both as if they were the eye in the midst of a whirling cyclone of activity.

"Because you needed me," Devlin finally answered before turning and making his way poolside again.

Leaving her with the unsettling thought that he was right. They had needed him. They needed him now.

So what would happen when his stint here was finished and he left for greener pastures?

FOR THE NEXT FEW DAYS, Michelle saw to it that Devlin barely had time to think. If he had been sent by her father to spy on her and undermine her wishes, she intended to see to it that the man was exposed to the truth. Worthington was sorely in need of repairs, but it wasn't on its last legs by a long shot.

While Wilson and Frieda Kleinschmidt lounged beneath an oak tree making sheep's eyes at one another, and her mother introduced the teens to the fine art of ethnic dances, Michelle had Devlin repair the plumbing, the staircase, and begin on the roof.

Stepping onto the back portico, she shielded her eyes with her hand and looked up to check on his progress.

He was nearly finished with the main slope of the center wing, but she grinned slightly to herself, knowing there was still plenty to do.

"Lemonade, Michelle?"

She glanced down to find Frieda beaming at her, her wizened face alight with excitement.

"No, thank you, Frieda."

"Then will you give this glass to your nice young man? Wilson and I thought we'd take a stroll."

Michelle absently took the glass, then glanced at Wilson, who was folding the lawn chairs they'd been using.

"I think he's taken a shine to you, Frieda."

Frieda blushed even more. "It's scandalous, I know. I shouldn't be carrying on with a younger man but..." She sighed in delight. "I can't help myself. One look at those muscular legs and I get all weak-kneed."

Michelle couldn't help the way her own gaze dropped to Wilson's knobby knees and spindly thighs. With the reddish tint he'd gained from his sunning sessions, he was giving a good impression of a flamingo in her estimation.

But then, she wasn't Frieda Kleinschmidt. And there was no accounting for attraction. It was something that often couldn't be explained.

As she watched the pair disappear through the garden gate, Michelle wondered if she would be so fortunate in her golden years. She could only pray she would have the health, strength and the attention of a good man to brighten her days.

Of their own accord, her eyes swung toward the roof again, taking in the figure who wore a pair of faded jeans, work boots, and a tool belt. Devlin had stripped to the waist some time ago, and the warm sun had already caused his skin to gleam with sweat.

My, oh my, oh my.

She would be a fool not to acknowledge that he had caught her attention at least once. How could she ignore him, especially when he'd abandoned his chores early in the day to take care of the meal preparation? More than once she'd unconsciously made her way into the kitchen on some halfhearted errand.

What was wrong with her? she wondered. She wasn't normally this obsessed with any man, let alone a servant.

But he was more than a servant, and therein lay the problem. If he was nothing more than her butler, she might chance the repercussions and allow their attraction to take its course. After all, this was the nineties and a woman couldn't be faulted for dating a coworker.

But her father had sent him. She was sure he'd sent him.

Her eyes widened as she saw him begin to back toward the lip of the roof. Her mouth grew dry as she watched him reach with his toe for the top of the ladder and she took a sip of the lemonade to ease the tightness.

He really did look great in a pair of jeans. His buttocks were tight and firm and . . .

Stop it!

She took another gulp, then tipped her chin at an imperious angle, doing her best to appear completely calm. When he turned to find her studying him, she asked, "So, how is it coming?"

He lifted a T-shirt from the tool chest, but rather than pulling it over his shoulders, he used it to wipe the sweat from his face and chest.

She shivered in a purely feminine response.

"I'll need more shingles."

"Fine. I'll order them this afternoon."

He nodded, holding out a hand. "Is that for me?"

She automatically gave the glass of lemonade to him, only then noting that it was half-gone.

He took it, then gazed at her consideringly. He didn't accuse her of drinking it, even though she knew he was sure just where most of it had gone.

Lifting the lemonade in silent salute, he downed the contents, causing her to watch as his Adam's apple slid up and down. Why such a simple thing intrigued her, she didn't know. But she found it hard to look away.

"What are you up to, Michelle?"

She started ever so slightly when he spoke.

"Up to?" she echoed weakly.

"The past few days you've been noticeably distant."

"Have I?"

"And you seem intent on having me complete every household repair by the end of the week."

"I couldn't think of any reason to delay."

"I see." He handed the glass back, but when she took it, he didn't immediately let go. "Then I guess my assumptions were wrong."

"What assumptions?" she asked weakly.

"That you were trying to avoid me. That you were trying to avoid this."

Before she could absorb his intent, he wrapped his free hand around her nape and pulled her to him. His kiss was hot, tasting of lemonade, sweat and man. The invasion of his tongue was complete, his hunger ravenous. Then he released her, causing her to stumble as she caught her balance.

"No, I don't suppose that's why you have me on top of the roof, is it, Michelle?" he asked. Then, to add insult to injury, his lips slid into a wide, all-knowing grin. Whistling softly, he returned to the ladder, hitched up his tool belt, and returned to his earlier position....

Leaving her quite shaky.

And quite aroused.

DEVLIN WAS FILLED with an inner pleasure as Michelle went out of her way to avoid him until dinnertime. He was sure that she would have made some excuse to keep from joining the group around the table, as well, if it wouldn't have caused so much attention.

As the teens settled into their places and he signed a greeting to Val, he surreptitiously studied Michelle, taking in the severe way she'd knotted her hair at the back of her head. Her face was all but devoid of makeup, her body clad in a pair of denim overalls and a T-shirt. Just by looking at her, Devlin knew he was meant to be anything but attracted to her.

But the plan backfired. She looked adorable, like someone caught playing dress-up.

For the past few days, Maude had encouraged the teenagers to try their hand at concocting some foreign delicacies from the cookbooks she'd ordered forwarded from her apartment, but Devlin had been in charge of this evening's meal. He was more than aware that Michelle had orchestrated the assignment and she meant to try to scare him off with the work to be done at Worthington, so he'd done his best to appear far from affected. Tonight, to show off his prowess at "whipping up" a gourmet meal, he'd planned to serve chicken piccata with a chocolate torte. Of course, the meal hailed from Don Guiseppe's Italian Villa in town and Wilson had been kind enough to pick it up on his way out with Frieda, but that wasn't something Devlin was about to spread around. As it was, he was going to have to dirty a few dishes to avoid suspicion.

The kids on KP duty had done an excellent job of setting the table, adding a festive centerpiece of marigolds—and a few dandelions—from the garden. Maude was wearing her best Chinese silk caftan, and even Jason was looking more lighthearted than usual—which could have been due to the fact that

Maude had been giving him driving lessons in the Rolls, insisting the van was too "uncool."

Taking his place at the foot of the table, Devlin joined hands with Willie and Kirk and bowed his head for grace.

A loud electronic shriek split the silence.

In an instant, Devlin leapt to his feet, rushing into the hallway, wondering which of the security wires had been tripped. It was at that instant, he saw a shadow race past the recreation room window.

Dashing out the front door, he ran to the side of the house, but by the time he'd reached the area where he'd seen the figure, whoever it was had gone.

"What's wrong?" Michelle shouted as she ran toward him.

Above her, one of the windows slid open. Seeing the huddle of teens behind her—Valerie especially pale— he pretended a nonchalance that he didn't feel.

"False alarm. A squirrel must have bumped one of the windows or something."

Bit by bit the kids dispersed, leaving only Michelle.

In the darkness he noted again that she looked like a kid playing dress-up with her scraped-back hair and businesslike clothes. Her eyes gleamed with apprehension and he could see that she was trembling.

"You're sure that's all it was? A squirrel?" she asked, her voice firm. But the way she'd tightly folded her arms beneath her breasts belied her nervousness.

He waved aside her concern. "I'm sure."

"You're lying, Mr. Rhett."

He sighed. This woman was far too astute for her own good.

Despite her bare feet, she padded toward him. "Did you find anything?" It was the first time he'd noted that she hadn't worn her shoes and there was something endearing about the fact. He found himself staring at the way her toes were curling into the grass. It was an unconscious, girlish gesture that made him want to smile. She was always trying to be so careful, to always be the adult in charge, but deep inside where it counted, she wasn't much different from her kids. She had street smarts and a wealth of knowledge, yet she was vulnerable.

"Some footprints," he answered, surprising even himself with his honesty. "But they're indistinct. Judging by the size, they could be a small man or a mature woman...or..."

"Or a kid," she finished for him. "Val's boyfriend has been forbidden to see her. Maybe he defied a court order and decided to pay her a visit?"

"There's no way to tell. But that's a possibility." He didn't tell her that there was another possibility. That someone had come to this place intent on her.

Arms still folded firmly beneath her chest, Michelle rocked back and forth on her feet. "It's quite a sticky situation. Her parents have signed over custody to foster care because she refuses to stay with them and keeps threatening to harm herself if they force her to live at home. Naturally, they worry about Val and want what's best for her. They're concerned for her safety, and they don't trust the boy who's done this to her, so they pulled a few strings with a judge, who's a friend of the family, and had her brought to Worthington.''

''How does Val feel about this?''

''Her caseworker thinks she's relieved to be taken out of the turmoil, even temporarily. She's furious at her parents for failing to understand her, yet she loves them too much to completely defy their wishes. Added to that is the fact that she and her boyfriend believe themselves to be in love, and nothing anybody says is going to convince them differently. Only time will tell who was ultimately right.''

''What about after the baby is born? Will she go back home to her parents?''

''I don't think anyone knows the answer to that question. But as long as she's underage, she can't be with Elliot.''

''How much longer before she *is* of age?''

''Four months.''

He walked toward her, slipping his jacket from his body and draping it over her shoulders. The October days had been hot as hell, but at night, it was easy to see that fall was in full swing. There was a definite nip to the air, one which her cotton T-shirt would not have the ability to block.

''Here.''

Reluctantly, she took it, then wriggled more firmly into its warmth.

"Thanks."

She began to walk in the direction of the pool, leaving the dewy wetness of the grass for the slate flagstones which still held a portion of the day's warmth.

"Maybe we should go in," he suggested.

"Not yet. Let the furor of the last few minutes settle down first."

A sweet silence settled over their shoulders and she stared up at the black sky, making Devlin follow her gaze. Bright diamond chips of starlight winked down at them. The moon was little more than a crooked grin to the east. Devlin couldn't remember the last time he'd taken the time to look up at such evening wonders.

"Tell me about yourself, Devlin Rhett," Michelle murmured.

"What's to tell?"

"I don't know. You're very secretive."

He shook his head. "There's nothing at all in my life that's a secret."

"So spill the beans. What is your family like? All I know is that your mother is British, your father American, and you have a kid brother who taught you sign language."

"There isn't much more to say. Mum and Dad met in the mid-fifties. It was love at first sight, or so they said. Even so, it was difficult for them. They wanted children, but it took years of trying before they had me. Six years later, they had another son, Ross. He was misdiagnosed as being mentally challenged until my mother brought him to a specialist in the United States. The strain of those years was probably too much for any marriage. Two years after moving to the States, my parents split up."

"What about you?"

"What about me?"

"What did you do when they divorced?"

"The usual rebellious things. I went to school, saw the world—"

"Became a butler."

He'd nearly forgotten that she thought he'd gone to some special school for training. Such a slip was enough to give him pause. He'd been so close to telling her everything, to exposing his true identity, and all because he'd begun to care for her in a very personal way.

Taking her arm, he turned her to face him. And once he'd touched her, he couldn't stop. His arms slipped around her waist, drawing her close.

"Don't ask any more questions," he whispered. "Don't make me think of the past or the future. All I have is this moment. The here and now."

Then he was drawing her against him, bending to brush his lips against hers, tasting the sweetness which had haunted him for days.

She didn't resist him. Her breath escaped in a soft sigh that caressed his cheek as her arms wrapped around his neck. She felt so good in his arms, so lithe and warm and real. Her breath was heady against his cheek, her mouth filled with infinite sweetness. Devlin gave in to the sensations, his hands roaming over her back and shoulders, exploring her body beneath the cover of his jacket.

Then, moments later, he forced himself to retreat. If he didn't, he knew that he wouldn't be able to stop at all.

"You'd better go inside."

But she didn't move.

And he couldn't seem to step away.

"If we stay out here like this, one of the kids will see us."

It was that pronouncement that finally forced her to move. She shifted away from him, automatically smoothing her hair into place.

"I don't like having this security system," she said, walking backward. "It makes me more apprehensive than I ever was without it."

"You'll get used to it," he assured her, knowing that he had to leave the garden, now, before he forgot why he was here.

Whoever had "visited" them tonight never should have got as far as the house, Devlin realized as an iciness invaded his limbs. If he'd been doing his job with his usual dispassionate concern, he wouldn't have been seated at that dinner table. He never would have taken his meals with Michelle and the kids. He would have been prowling the halls and doing his job.

Sighing in disgust at his own carelessness, Devlin headed toward the front door, ignoring the way Michelle watched him with wide hurt eyes. He knew she was unconsciously begging for his reassurance, but that wasn't something he could give. Not until he drew the reins on his own wayward emotions.

Forcing himself to think of the job, only the job, he told himself he would wait until later to thoroughly examine the area beneath the window where he'd seen the figure. Until then, he would hold his tongue. Michelle was already as tense as a cat, and he didn't want to tip her off to the fact that her own life was being threatened.

He'd taken several steps when he heard Michelle following him in the darkness. He prayed silently that she would keep the distance between them, that her pace wouldn't quicken, that she wouldn't reach out and touch him.

Bloody hell, how he wanted her to touch him. That afternoon, it had been all he could do to push her from his mind long enough to work. But now, after kissing her, caressing her, no matter how briefly, her nearness was all but impossible to ignore.

Think of the job. Only the job.

He spun to face her so quickly, she didn't have time to adjust her steps, and she crashed into him headlong. His arms snapped around her waist to steady her, then lingered there.

It was then, looking down into her wide, guileless eyes, that he knew he'd made a mistake in coming to Worthington. This wasn't a woman to be trifled with. She was the sort a man protected, cherished. The sort he didn't offer to involve in an affair, but in marriage. She was . . .

Perfect.

Perfect in every way but one.

She could never settle for a man like him. One who made his living from violence, who'd left a half-dozen disastrous relationships in his wake. He didn't belong in her world where life was orderly and meals were served at the same time each day.

Reluctantly, he let her go for the second time that evening.

"Good night, Michelle."

Without offering an explanation for his odd behavior, he turned and made his way into the kitchen, knowing he didn't belong with the rest of the family in the dining hall.

Family?

His brain screeched to a halt at that thought, but it was true. The occupants of Worthington might be considered unorthodox by those who didn't know them better, but there was no doubting they were a family. He would be wise to remember that even though he might sit at the head of the table...

He wasn't their father.

Chapter Nine

"Valerie, it's time for your birthing class."

The reminder automatically popped from Michelle's lips before she caught the absurdity of the call. She was so accustomed to shouting through the house when she needed something of her kids that it hadn't dawned on her that the teenager she was calling to was deaf.

"You're losing your mind, Michelle," she mumbled to herself, gathering her purse and keys and going in search of the girl.

Instead of Valerie, however, it was Devlin she found first. He was waiting in the vestibule, leaning back against the table, his feet crossed at the ankles and his hands propped on the wood behind him.

She came to a sudden halt, one that was completely telling. But she couldn't help it. This man had the ability to disconcert her in more ways than she'd ever known possible, and this morning was no exception.

He was wearing a pair of elegant dress pants with a banded collar shirt tucked into his waist. He'd rolled the cuffs to his forearms exposing muscular flesh, tanned to a golden brown.

"Val will be right down," he said when she didn't speak. "She forgot her pillow."

Michelle nodded, clearing her throat so that she could speak with some semblance of normalcy. "I appreciate your willingness to serve as her interpreter during her class."

He shrugged. "No problem."

The silence settled between them, growing warm and sticky.

"Is the van ready to go?"

He nodded.

"What about the rest of the kids?" Six of the teenagers would be going with them to the clinic for their yearly sports physicals.

"They're already on board and adjusting the radio."

She grimaced. "One can only hope they'll find the classical station."

"Dream on."

The squeak of the stairs signaled that Valerie had arrived. She waddled down to the main floor, gripping the railing in one hand and her pillow in the other.

Using what little sign language she knew, Michelle greeted her with, "Good morning," speaking aloud at the same time as she'd been instructed so that Val could read her lips. "Are you ready?" she asked.

Val nodded.

Gesturing for them all to head outside, Michelle shouted to the occupants who would be staying behind, "Don't let the place burn down while we're gone!"

As they approached the van, Michelle winced. The vehicle was already shaking to a thunderous selection of rap music, the swaying motions increased even more by the wild gyrations the teens were making to the omnipresent rhythm of the drums.

"Turn it down," Michelle ordered over the din as she helped Valerie climb into the front seat.

"We've got to have it loud," Willie insisted.

"Why?"

"So Val can feel the beat."

Michelle rolled her eyes. "The whole block can feel the beat. Turn it down."

It was Jason who bent between the two front seats to adjust the volume to a more tolerable level. Then, as Michelle climbed into the van beside the boy and slammed the door, Devlin revved the engine.

Less than five minutes later, they were pulling to a stop at the local clinic. Before she opened the door, Michelle issued her instructions.

"Val, you'll be going with Mr. Rhett."

Devlin signed to her even though she was watching Michelle's lips.

"The rest of you will come with me to see Dr. Francom. I'm estimating that it will take at least an hour, maybe two, for all of you to be examined and get your certificates. Where will you be afterward?"

They grimaced at her drill-sergeant tone.

"On the basketball court in the park next door," they replied in unison. Even Devlin hid a smile and Michelle realized she'd probably asked the same question a dozen times en route.

"Excellent."

She turned to Devlin. "The two of you will be in room—"

"Two-eleven," Devlin interrupted. "We know."

"I'll be there as soon as—"

"You have everyone settled."

Realizing she was providing far too much amusement for the day, Michelle yanked open the door and slid out. She waited until everyone had emerged and the car was locked, before leading her own flock toward the sliding doors.

Behind her, she could hear Jason lazily dribbling his ball as he, Willie, Kirk, Jessica, Marie and Rusty followed her into the rambling building.

She led the way down a twisting set of corridors to a door on the far end of the east wing. Holding it open, she waved them inside. "After you."

It took nearly twenty minutes to register the kids, fill out all the various forms required, then inform the nurse where she could be found if needed. As she hurried back toward room 211, she realized that the birthing class would be well under way.

Slipping in through the rear door, she dropped her purse on the floor and pushed the sleeves of her sweater to her elbows.

She'd been expecting to find various couples supine on the floor practicing their breathing exercises. Instead, hearing a round of laughter, she glanced up and stared.

A table had been drawn up in front of a rolling chalkboard. A blanket covered the hard wooden surface, giving it the appearance of a bed. Devlin's lean frame reclined in the middle, his head and shoulders propped up with pillows. Somewhere in the direction of his midsection, a lumpy shape had been hidden beneath his sweater.

"Now, in review . . ." the instructor intoned.

Devlin translated the words into sign language for Val, who sat in a nearby seat.

"These are the breathing exercises for expulsion."

Again, Devlin translated.

"Take two deep breaths. Inhale . . . exhale. Inhale . . . exhale."

While he gave the information to Valerie, Devlin's chest rose and fell as he demonstrated.

"On the third breath, you will inhale, then hold."

The instructor grasped Devlin's shoulders, forcing him forward. "Make a rounded arch of your shoulders and spine, keeping your lungs full of air. Tighten the muscles of your abdomen and tilt your pelvic region.''

Michelle had to choke back a laugh as Devlin complied.

''Bear down, down, down, always remembering that you are pushing the baby.''

The woman patted the protrusion beneath Devlin's shirt and a tiny plastic hand dropped out. Apologizing, she covered it again, causing Devlin to chuckle and his breath to escape in a whoosh.

The other occupants present joined in the merriment until the instructor raised her hands in a bid for silence.

''You should maintain pushing as long as you can, but when you exhale, do it slowly. As soon as you can, begin the process again.''

Devlin complied, although his shoulders continued to shake.

''You will proceed in the same manner until the contraction ends. Then, take cleansing breaths and rest so that you'll be ready to begin the process again for the next contraction.''

Michelle sat in one of the folding chairs positioned at the back of the room, watching as Val asked a question and Devlin clarified.

''At home, I want you to practice these procedures in the positions I explained earlier. Always keep in mind that such techniques will allow you to give birth to a healthy, happy baby.''

With that, she whipped the doll from beneath Devlin's shirt, wrapped it in a blanket, and laid it on his chest. "Congratulations, Mr. Rhett." Looking up at the group, she said, "Let's give him a hand for being our guinea pig."

Michelle added her own applause to that of the couples present, feeling a tug of tenderness somewhere near her heart as Devlin swung from the table and rejoined Val—still carrying the doll in the crook of his arm.

For some reason, her eyes clung to that last image and the memory of it became etched in her brain. Unaccountably, she found herself wondering if Devlin wanted children. He would make a good father. She knew that from the way he interacted with her kids. But to see him with a baby...

Wrenching her thoughts away from such a dangerous track, she blinked as the lights were extinguished.

"Now, for the event you've all been waiting for. A film of an actual delivery."

The instructor rolled a trolley filled with video equipment to the front of the room and pushed the play button with more relish than was necessary.

Since Devlin already had things well in hand, Michelle stood and crept from the room. A tenuous bond of trust was forming between Val and the hard-jawed butler, and Michelle thought it would be best if the girl didn't sense her presence. It was important that she know that Michelle trusted him to see to Val's needs.

Trusted him, her mind echoed as she walked into the hall and took a seat on one of the low waiting-room chairs.

Yes, she trusted him. He may have come to her under peculiar circumstances—and she might still want a few explanations in regard to his mysterious employer—but she had no qualms about his being at Worthington. He had proven to be an asset to their program. In fact, she found herself dreading the moment when his service would be finished. He would leave then. Just as every other man she'd learned to care about had left.

The door to the classroom whispered open, and she looked up, surprised to find Devlin easing into the hallway. She was about to speak to him when he braced his buttocks against the wall and leaned forward, taking deep gulping breaths.

She laughed out loud, causing his head to jerk up.

"Couldn't take the movie, huh?"

"No. Thank heavens for closed captioning."

She patted the chair beside her. "Then come take a load off your feet." Michelle gestured to the television bolted to the wall above her. "PBS is hosting a marathon of nature movies."

He straightened, peering around the corner. As soon as he saw the screen, he blanched. The cameraman had just zoomed in for a close-up of a zebra giving birth.

Groaning, he didn't say another word. He merely dragged his fingers through his hair, pulled a sucker from his breast pocket, and made his way back into the Lamaze room.

MICHELLE WATCHED the other couples file into the hall one by one, then the instructor.

Gathering her bag, she waited for Devlin and Val to appear, but the corridor soon lapsed into a quiet abandonment.

Frowning, she wondered if she'd missed them somehow, then shook her head. There hadn't been that many people for her to confuse strangers for Val and Devlin. Besides, she seemed to have an automatic homing instinct where Devlin was concerned, and it hadn't gone off.

Sighing, she checked her watch, then peered inside the room. He and Val were near the front of the room, their chairs facing one another, their heads bent close. Michelle was about to speak, but something about the low tone of Devlin's voice informed her that the conversation he was holding with Val was intense and important.

"Maybe you should cut Elliot some slack."

Val's fingers flashed.

"I know he's got it easy, but not entirely. He wants to be with you. He wants to be there when the baby is born."

Val's expression was mutinous as she responded.

"True, he shouldn't have insulted your parents, and he shouldn't have made things difficult for you at home."

Her hands moved with balletlike grace in the near-darkness.

"I know they think he's a hooligan, but the two of you aren't going to convince them any differently by the way you've been acting."

Michelle didn't need to guess what her corresponding gesture meant.

"Pretty talk," he murmured with a crooked grin. "But you've got to admit that trashing the house and attempting to run away to Reno wasn't the best way to win their approval."

Her face fell.

"Val, I want you to look at this situation from your parents' point of view."

When she would have made a furious response, he held her hands until she grew calmer. Then, he pressed her palms against her rounded stomach before saying, "It will only be a few weeks and this little guy will be turning to you for help. I know you love him. You haven't even met him yet, but he's stolen your heart in a way that no one else will ever do. Already, you would do anything to protect him and ensure his happiness. Wouldn't you?''

She nodded.

''Now I want you to think what it will be like sixteen, seventeen years from now when he brings home a woman with three earrings, a pierced nose and blue hair. She has no job, no prospects, she's been with a biker gang for the better part of three years. You've done everything you can to make your son happy and this stranger he's brought to meet you seems determined to rip him away so that you'll never see him again.''

Her chin wobbled.

''Wouldn't you do exactly what your parents have done with you? Wouldn't you find a safe place for him to live, then do everything in your power so he doesn't see that girl until his head has cleared?''

She reluctantly agreed, then flashed a question of her own.

''I don't know, Val,'' he said with a sigh. ''But I think you're selling your relationship with Elliot short. If what the two of you are experiencing is love, really and truly, how can a couple of months really hurt?''

Her fingers flew.

''Give your parents a chance. Let them see that you're trying to meet them halfway. That might be all it takes to show them that you're thinking with a level head.''

She responded.

"Well, if it doesn't work, at least you'll know you've tried."

Her eyes filled with tears and he drew her into his arms, pressing her cheek into the crook of his shoulder. As he rocked her, soothed her, Michelle ducked back into the hall. Leaning her back against the wall, she blinked at the moisture that had gathered in her own eyes.

Damn man, she inwardly groused. *He wasn't supposed to make her cry, too.*

She sniffled and made her way to the drinking fountain, sipping the frigid water, then splashing it on her face.

"We're all done here. Val's gone back to the van."

She jumped, whirling to find Devlin standing behind her. He was so close that all she had to do was lift her hand to touch him.

But she couldn't.

She mustn't.

"Good." The word stuck in her throat and she cleared it. "Good, let's head back to the van."

He caught her before she could take more than two steps.

"What's wrong?"

"Nothing." But the response broke in the middle.

Damn it all, she was going to start crying again.

Devlin's expression became fierce. "What's happened? What's wrong?"

"Nothing." The word was punctuated with a sniffle.

"Michelle, please, what's wrong?"

A sound broke from her throat, one that was half sob, half chortle. "Not a damned thing, Mr. Rhett." She waved in the general direction of the classroom. "That was just so sweet."

This time, it was his turn to look uncomfortable. "You heard, huh?"

She laughed again. "I heard *your* half of it."

He offered a grin, then grew serious. "I hope I wasn't out of line by talking to her like that."

"No. I think what you said was very sound advice. She trusts you, so maybe she'll give some thought to your ideas. From what I understand, she's always been very close to her parents. I think she misses them more than she's willing to admit. If there's any way to resolve this situation without Val and Elliot running off together as soon as she's eighteen, everyone will be happier, I'm sure."

He still hadn't removed his hand from her arm. Firmly, resolutely, he pulled her closer to him.

"What about you, Michelle?"

Her brow furrowed. "What about me?"

"Val isn't the only member of Worthington who suffers from a good deal of angst whenever her parents are mentioned."

Michelle immediately stiffened. "I get along very well with my mother."

"I'm not talking about your mother."

She glared at him. "I don't think my father is any of your business."

"I'm sure that's true, but I'd hate to think that you'll spend the rest of your life looking over your shoulder for paternal conspiracies."

Her lips thinned. "You know nothing about my relationship with my father."

"No, but I do know that you won't talk to him, that you won't let him help you."

"*Help me!* The only way he wishes to help is to push me back into the role of a perfect socialite hostess."

"So instead of showing him what you do, how much passion you have for helping these kids of yours, you've closed him off completely."

She remained mulishly silent.

He stepped closer, framing her face with his hands.

"Give him a chance, Michelle. Show him that you're good at what you do."

"You *were* sent by Daddy, weren't you?"

"No."

For the first time, she believed him.

"No, I wasn't sent here by your father. But I want you to be happy."

She felt the prickling of tears for the second time that day.

"I don't think you'll ever be truly content, feel truly independent and free, until you've resolved this argument."

"Why should it matter to you, how I feel?"

He hesitated, bending toward her. "Because I care about you," he finally admitted. "More than I ever should."

Then he was kissing her, and it was as if she were a seed awakened from a drought. Her arms slid around his neck and she lifted on tiptoe, needing to erase the last shred of distance between them.

His arms swept around her waist, lifting her to him. A pure wave of ecstasy flooded her body, as if she'd been admitted into heaven after first experiencing hell. And for the first time, she allowed herself to admit the truth about herself, about this man. She didn't want to resist him anymore. She didn't want to pretend that he didn't affect her, that she didn't...

Care about him, too.

The idea was so sudden that she broke free, staring up at him in surprise.

Yes. She did care about him. Not just physically. No, she might melt the moment he touched her, but that wasn't the only thing that drew her to him. He fed her emotionally and spiritually. He had awakened parts of her she hadn't known existed and he'd made her feel *alive*.

She touched his cheek, ran her thumb over his bottom lip. "Devlin, I..."

A low wolf whistle slid into the silence. Then a round of sporadic clapping caused her to glance over her shoulder.

Heat scalded her cheeks as she took in the tableau before her—her teenagers staring her way, grinning and whispering amongst themselves.

But even as she heard Devlin's whispered curse, she grew calm and serene. Maybe it was time that her kids saw the makings of a healthy relationship, one based on trust and honesty and mutual affection.

Deftly slipping from Devlin's grasp, she threw her kids a cocky grin and ordered, "Out to the car."

Then she sauntered past her audience with complete self-assurance, knowing that she'd done the right thing.

DEVLIN WAS PUTTING the linens away in the upper hall closet, when he heard the whispers coming from Val and Annie's room.

"I think we should do something nice for her. Look what she's done for us."

Curious, he glanced around the edge of the doorframe. When he realized that all of the teenagers of Worthington were having a powwow, he paused.

Annie was obviously holding court since the rest of the group had gathered around her bed.

"Cough it up," she said, holding out her hand.

One by one, the teenagers around her emptied their pockets and tossed their hard-earned allowances onto the center of the quilt.

Val had obviously been put in charge of finances because she counted the change, then scribbled a total on a yellow pad.

"Great. Thirty-two dollars and sixteen cents," Annie announced. "Now we need some ideas. Where should we send them on a date?"

Devlin's brow furrowed as suggestions were bandied back and forth. It wasn't until they'd decided upon a modest restaurant in the center of town that he realized these kids were talking about Michelle and him.

Grinning, he backed away, intent on giving them their privacy. But halfway down the staircase, the smile faded.

A date. As in, he and Michelle alone. By themselves. No kids. No distractions.

He frowned. He would have to put a stop to it. He'd sworn to himself that he wouldn't allow his own feelings to get in the way of his job. Not again. No.

But even as he turned, he found he didn't have the heart to break up their meeting. He kept remembering the way they'd turned their pockets inside out and dumped the change in the middle of the bed.

A sigh lifted his chest and he shook his head.

Damn, what a mess. He couldn't refuse their offer. He couldn't ruin such a spontaneous, unselfish gesture from these kids. It wouldn't be right. It wouldn't be fair. He would have to go out with Michelle. He would have to enjoy himself. He would have to see to it that they both had a good time.

Damn, what a mess.

But this time, as he made his way downstairs, he couldn't quite tamp down the grin that pulled at the corners of his lips.

Chapter Ten

An electronic shriek brought Devlin out of his bed and reaching for his revolver before conscious thought had an opportunity to strike. Whipping open his door, he raced down the corridor, his eyes automatically checking windows and doors as he went.

Making his way to the front of the house, he caught sight of a shadow crossing the front yard.

"Stay where you are!" he shouted to the teenagers gathering at the top of the staircase.

Within seconds, he'd jerked open the front door and beaten a path after the fleeing intruder, knowing that if the suspect made it to the front gate, he would probably escape unhindered since Devlin was without shoes—not to mention, all but without clothes except for his sweatpants.

Then, miracle of miracles, the man tripped, and went sprawling face first. As Devlin raced toward him, tackling the shape again when he tried to jump up, he saw a baseball bat lying concealed in the grass.

Thank you, Willie, he said to himself as he threw the figure to the ground and pointed the revolver at his head.

"Who are you?" he growled, shoving the barrel of the gun into the kid's cheek.

Then, it struck him. It was a kid. A *kid.*

And he was scared to death.

Devlin's grip loosened infinitesimally, although he maintained a secure handhold of his shirt.

"Who are you?" he demanded again.

"Elliot Grover."

Devlin grew still, recognizing the name.

"Listen, mister, I only wanted to see Val. She's having my baby, y'know?"

Devlin cursed under his breath. "Why didn't you wait until morning and knock on the door like everyone else?"

"'Cause her parents have got a court order against me. If I get caught talking to her, they'll put me in jail."

Shoving the revolver into the back of his waistband, Devlin rose, reached down, and yanked the boy up by the collar. "Well, you might end up in jail yet."

Elliot's eyes widened and his lips trembled. "But I didn't mean to scare anybody."

"Scare, hell, you set off an alarm system. Did you actually think that wouldn't alert somebody that you were here?"

"I didn't think the place was wired."

Devlin rolled his eyes, knowing that the boy had to be telling the truth. Anyone who might have been hired to hurt Michelle would surely be savvy enough to know the obvious signs of a security system.

"Come on." He kept a firm grasp on the kid's arm, leading him in the direction of the driveway.

"Are you taking me to see Val?"

"Hell, no. You've got an injunction against you, remember?"

"Oh." It was clear that Elliot had hoped he would have forgotten.

"What's the limit? How far away do you have to stay?"

"A hundred feet."

"Then we'll head out by the curb. You and I are going to have a talk."

As soon as Michelle saw Devlin streaking out the door, she shepherded her charges back into their rooms, then made a call to 911. By the time she'd pulled a pair of jeans under her oversize sleep shirt and laced herself into a set of sneakers, she could see that Devlin had caught the intruder and was leading him to the front curb.

Rushing onto the front stoop, she was ready to join him on the grass when Devlin waved her away.

"Give me a minute," he shouted.

Give him a minute? *Give* him a minute?

She opened her mouth to protest, but he'd already turned his back on her. To add insult to injury, his hand cupped the perpetrator's shoulder in a way that was...supportive? Friendly?

Michelle folded her arms under her breasts, a small harrumph of frustration bursting from her lips. Her butler was getting awfully chummy with an attempted burglar, in her opinion.

But that was nothing compared to what she had yet to see. In the amount of time it took for her to hear police sirens in the distance, she saw the two of them engage in what looked like a heart-to-heart conversation. Then, the intruder broke down, began to sob, and Devlin comforted him.

At that point, Michelle would have gone out to join them, no matter what Devlin had said, but when the police car appeared, lights flashing, she thought it might be best to stay put. Let Devlin explain what had happened. Let him explain why he'd chased this character into the night and then had become his best friend.

In less than five minutes, the police car was leaving with the suspect ensconced in the front seat—not in handcuffs as she had hoped, but riding free as he pleased as if he were some sort of guest.

As Devlin began walking back to the front door, her toe began to beat an impatient tattoo on the polished hardwood. By the time he'd made it to the top step, she was in a full-fledged snit.

"Just what was happening out there?" she demanded as he stepped inside.

He didn't answer her directly. "Where are the kids?"

"Upstairs in their rooms."

"Asleep?"

"I doubt it. I'm sure that they had their noses pressed against the window and witnessed the same incredible display I did."

He arched one brow at her tone and she took a deep breath, knowing that it would do her no good if she sounded hysterical.

"Did you know that person?"

He shook his head. "No."

"Then why were you on such...*friendly* terms with him?"

"We talked, that's all. I was able to discover that he wasn't on any sort of a nefarious agenda, he just wanted to visit with one of the kids."

"Then why didn't he come during daylight hours and use the front door like any reasonable person would have done?"

"He was sure you wouldn't let him in."

"Is he some sort of criminal or something?"

"No."

"Then why wouldn't I let him in?" she demanded again.

Devlin studied her carefully, as if he didn't trust her reaction to what he might say. Then, flicking a glance toward the top of the stairs, he said, "Come on. Let's go somewhere a little more . . . private."

She was about to retort that he needn't be so dramatic, when she heard the slight squeak of a floorboard overhead and realized that they were probably being spied upon.

"Fine. Lead the way."

He strode past her, making his way down the hall which led to the kitchen and his own room. As she followed, she couldn't seem to avoid noting the breadth of his bare shoulders, the strength of his spine, the . . .

"Is that a gun?" she demanded, stopping short.

She stared at the bulge in the back of his sweatpants, unable to ignore the gleam of a very lethal-looking pistol butt that poked out of the waistband.

"Yeah, why?"

He reached behind him to grasp the weapon and slide it free from his clothing, but he didn't alter his pace.

"You brought a *gun* into my *home?*"

This time, her disbelief must have transmitted itself to him because he turned to face her.

"You seem upset."

"Seem? *Seem?*" She couldn't believe what she was hearing. "I don't *seem* upset—I *am* upset."

"Why?"

Michelle was nearly sputtering, she was so angry. "This is a home for troubled teenagers. The last thing

I need is for you to bring in a loaded weapon." She glanced at it again, muttering, "I'm assuming it *is* loaded."

"Of course it is. I'd hardly be waving around a squirt gun, now would I?"

"I wish you were."

"Why? I assure you, I keep track of the pistol at all times."

It took her a moment to absorb the import of what he was saying, but when she did, she balled her hands into fists. "Do you mean you've had that...that... *thing* on your... person this whole time? That you've been carrying it around? That it hasn't been hidden under your pillow or something?"

"Sure."

She could have punched him in the stomach, but judging by the hardness of his abdomen, she didn't think that would relieve her stress.

Knowing she had to put some distance between them to keep from launching into orbit, she spun on her heel, stalked several feet away, then whirled again, jabbing an accusing finger into the air.

"Why would you feel it necessary to *arm* yourself in order to work here?"

"Have you taken a good look at the neighborhood? It's not exactly Happy Valley out there."

"But it's not Beirut, either."

"As a butler, it's my responsibility to see to the safety of the occupants of this house."

"Where did you get that idea?"

"From you."

She opened her mouth, then closed it again when she realized he was right to some extent. She had asked him to see to the security system.

But she had never dreamed he'd go this far!

"I asked you to install an electronic alarm, not carry a revolver around beneath your shirt."

"I hid it under my trousers, actually."

She was not about to ask him where.

"No," she stated firmly, then added to her objection by waving her hands in front of her like a football referee. "No, no, no. I will not have it. You will get rid of that thing. I want it off the premises by tomorrow morning or you're out of here, no matter what your anonymous donor and my board of directors might say."

His lips pressed together, then he nodded. "Fine. You have my word."

She took several deep breaths, certain that he'd agreed far too easily.

"I will not be bucked on this issue," she warned. "If I find out that you've—"

"I've given my word. That should be enough."

It was apparent that she'd insulted him by distrusting his promise, but it wasn't something she would apologize for doing. Not when so much was at stake. She would not compromise the safety of her charges. Nor would she condone the use of firearms.

In her opinion, there were already too many teen-agers who felt that the use of guns and knives was a superior means of handling their problems.

"I've given my word, Michelle. It will have to be enough," Devlin said when she didn't immediately respond.

"Trust him, dear, I do."

Michelle spun around to discover Maude had been eavesdropping on the entire conversation. "Moth-er—"

"I know, I know. This is a...private discussion." She offered a coy smile and waggled her fingers. "Good night. To the both of you."

For several seconds after her mother had gone, Michelle's body hummed with tension, but then the adrenaline pumping through her system eased. She trusted him and knew he understood her point, so there was nothing more to be said. "Very well."

Her pulse was slowly regaining a more normal rhythm. "Come with me, please," she ordered, slap-ping her hand against the kitchen door.

"For what?"

"Coffee. I think we could both use some."

She snapped on the light and began preparing the brew, all the time completely aware of the man who followed her, took a seat at the table, then set the re-volver on the tabletop. When she turned to study him, he'd leaned back in his chair and extended his legs.

"Is that thing still loaded?" She waved indirectly toward the gun.

He cradled it in his palm, removing the clip and holding it out to her. "Do you want this?"

She supposed it was a challenge of sorts, but if so, it was one she would fail. In the matter of her kids, there could be no halfhearted efforts in looking after their welfare.

"I'll just put it out of the way for now, then you can take it with you when we've finished."

Lifting the clip as if it were a dead rat, she set it on top of the refrigerator.

"Do you think that's far enough away from the pistol?" he asked, his brows rising and a distinct twinkle settling in the blue depths of his eyes.

She didn't rise to the bait, but leaned her hips against the counter and crossed her ankles.

"So, why did you send the police away?"

"They agreed with me that it would be best if we didn't press charges."

Michelle wanted to argue that there was no "we" involved in decision making at Worthington, but the image of the way he'd sat on the curb, talking to the boy, holding him as he wept, stopped her.

"What made you think that?"

Instead of answering her, Devlin countered her question with one of his own. "Do you know who he was?"

"No."

"That's the father of Valerie's baby."

Michelle wasn't quite sure what she was supposed to say to that. Luckily, the machine behind her was beginning to dribble coffee into the pot and she was able to buy time by busying herself with gathering mugs, sugar and milk.

"Did you know that there's a restraining order against him?" she asked, setting the cups on the table.

"Yes. He told me."

Michelle stared at him. "He *told* you?"

"I think it was the barrel of a gun in his face that convinced him to open a dialogue."

"So, what did he want?"

"To see the girl."

She offered a curt sigh. "He can't do that."

"I explained that fact to him. He's agreed to stay away."

"And you believed him?"

"Yes."

"Why?"

"Because he knows that if he tries something like this again, I'll be after him like a tick on a hound."

The response caused her lips to twitch. "A tick on a hound, huh? Somehow, that doesn't sound very British."

"I'm only half English. My father was from Tennessee."

"That explains it."

Michelle settled into a chair, drinking her own coffee black. She needed her wits about her and she was hoping that the coffee would help to bring them to full attention.

"So, what did the two of you talk about during your heart-to-heart chat?"

"Fatherhood."

The blunt answer took her by surprise.

"Oh, really," she drawled. "And what would you know about such a subject, Mr. Rhett?"

He took a sip of his own drink, then stared down into the dark depths of his cup as if it were a crystal ball.

"I was married once."

Michelle felt a twinge of shock—although why, she didn't know. She knew so little about this man.

"You have children?" she asked, unsure why her throat had become so tight.

He shook his head. "My marriage was not a... comfortable one."

She didn't know what to say to that, but he didn't appear to need a response.

"The first few years weren't bad. We were both busy, both working hard at our own careers. I don't think we even noticed that on those rare occasions we had some time alone together, we had nothing to talk about."

"What happened?"

"Nan was on birth control, something we both strongly insisted upon. Looking back on it now, I think that, subconsciously, we both knew the relationship wasn't going to work. Anyway, when she began showing the signs of pregnancy, we were shocked. We hadn't planned on a baby. Our lives didn't allow for a child." He grimaced. "It made me take a good, long look at myself and where I was headed." His mouth twisted in a self-deprecating manner. "I didn't much like what I saw."

The silence of the room settled around them, tense and expectant.

"The baby?" Michelle finally asked when she couldn't bear the mystery any longer.

"It was a false alarm. They discovered that Nan had a cyst that was mimicking the signs of pregnancy."

The tension that had mysteriously invaded Michelle's body eased ever so slightly.

"You must have been relieved."

He grimaced. "Actually... no."

She noted the way he continued to stare into his coffee as if he were afraid of what she might see if she looked too deeply into his eyes.

"When they told me, I felt as if I'd lost something. At that instant, everything I'd thought and said and worried about swam into focus and I realized that my objections to the pregnancy hadn't been based on the fact that I didn't want a child, but that I wanted one so much it scared me."

His words left an echo of themselves in her mind, reminding her of her own reaction to her broken engagement. She knew now that she hadn't regretted the fact that Steven had left her, but that in doing so, all of the plans she'd made had become null and void.

"You told all this to that boy?"

"Elliot," he supplied. "His name is Elliot." He drank deeply, then confirmed, "We didn't get this far into my relationship with my ex-wife, but I did talk to him about how frightening it can be to contemplate being a father."

"Not as frightening as contemplating thirty hours of labor."

He grinned. "Maybe not. But sometimes I think so much attention is lavished on the mother-to-be that we forget there's a father-to-be as well. He's inundated with worries about his wife, about the baby, about the future, and about his own role in it all. Yet, men aren't encouraged to talk about such things, there are no support groups or classes for what they're going through. They're expected to remain stoic and cool."

Michelle could see now why Elliot had broken down and why he'd allowed Devlin to comfort him. He must have been feeling much the same emotions Devlin had expressed, but had also been forced to deal with a restraining order which kept him away from Val and his unborn baby.

"You're a very good man, Mr. Rhett."

At her low comment, one of his brows rose. Michelle could tell that the statement had taken him by surprise—and had even embarrassed him slightly.

"There aren't many people who would take the time to talk to someone like Elliot. They would merely brand him a hellion and send him off with the police."

She cringed inside when she realized that she'd echoed her own first reaction. The whole situation reminded her that she was far from perfect when it came to handling troubled teenagers.

Rhett's eyes had darkened, fixing on her face with an intensity which was far more sensual than it should have been considering the current topic of conversation. She wondered if he knew how much power he had over her with a single gaze. So much so that she could no longer hold back her praise.

"You've been an asset to Worthington."

He didn't respond, and she was glad. By remaining silent, he showed her that the compliment had touched him in some small way.

"They're a good group of kids," he said much later when the silence threatened to go on too long.

At that moment, Michelle wished he would stay at Worthington, that he would slip into the role of a male protector and adviser. As well as . . .

What?

Why couldn't she be honest with herself? Why couldn't she admit that she wanted him to stay for purely selfish reasons?

"Michelle?"

They both jumped when Annie spoke to them from the doorway.

"Yes, Annie?"

"Was that Val's boyfriend?"

It was Devlin who responded. "Yes."

"Did the police arrest him?"

"No. They're going to give him a ride."

Annie's shoulders sagged from their defensive posture, conveying that she'd already become Val's confidante. "Good . . . well . . . good night."

The kitchen door flapped behind her retreating figure and Michelle started when Devlin took her hand.

"I think I should warn you that your kids are cooking up some kind of date for the two of us."

"What?" The word was barely audible, escaping on a puff of air.

"I overheard them making plans. They were shelling out their money and dumping it into a pile on the middle of the bed when I walked past."

Michelle's heart had begun to pound again, but this time from something other than fear. She'd never dreamed that her kids would do such a thing. In fact, she'd anticipated little more than a rash of teasing after being caught in Mr. Rhett's embrace.

But a date? The gesture was so sweet, so giving, so...

Awful.

She couldn't possibly go on a date with Devlin Rhett. They would be alone together in an entirely intimate situation. If Michelle could barely keep her thoughts and yearnings in line now, how would she manage hours upon end of Devlin's undiluted personality?

Devlin must have read her hesitation because he wound his fingers through hers and squeezed. "We can't disappoint them."

Michelle opened her mouth to object. But as his thumb grazed her skin, she stopped herself just in time.

Why not? Why not spend one evening with this man? He would leave them all one day, and if she didn't take the risk now, if she didn't learn just how far the emotions between them had developed, she would regret being so cautious.

She deserved this, her conscience asserted. She deserved one wild, spontaneous evening with Devlin Rhett.

"I would be pleased to spend some time with you, Mr. Rhett," she said, her voice much softer and silkier than she'd intended.

Then, standing, she extricated herself from his grasp, knowing that the time had come for her to leave. If she didn't, she wouldn't be able to do so.

She put her mug in the sink, feeling his gaze every step of the way. Only at the door did she hesitate. Reaching on top of the refrigerator, she located the clip, turned, and tossed it his way.

He caught it purely by reflex. "You'll go?"

"Sure. Let me know what they plan for us so I'll know what to wear."

Then she was heading into the hall, her step jaunty, her spirit lighter than it had been in decades.

Chapter Eleven

Michelle felt like a teenager herself as she slid a pair of dangling pearl earrings into her ears, then stood back from the mirror to check the result.

"You look hot, Michelle," Jessica stated.

"Thanks."

"Turn around so we can see," Sammy ordered.

Michelle did as she was told, a trifle embarrassed by her attire. For the better part of an hour, the girls at Worthington had been "dressing" Michelle for her upcoming date with Mr. Rhett. They'd fixed her hair, painted her nails, then raided her closet for something "hot."

Upon encountering the loose sweaters, simple dresses, and racks of jeans and shorts, Annie had rushed to her own room and returned with the black bandage dress she'd worn to the senior prom the year before.

Seeing the short, skintight dress, Michelle had done her best to talk them all into letting her choose something else, but none of the girls would hear of it.

"He's seen you in all those kinds of clothes, Michelle," Sammy insisted. "You have to look romantic."

Gazing at her reflection in the mirror hung on the door of her walk-in closet, Michelle wasn't sure if *romantic* was the word she would use to describe herself. Her hair had been swept to one side and tumbled over her shoulder in a riot of curls. The makeup the teens had employed was surprisingly subtle, causing her eyes to appear dark and enigmatic and her skin to adopt a rose-tinted flush. Below that, the dress left her arms and shoulders bare. Slender spaghetti straps led to a dress that cloaked her figure like a layer of ink, ending at a spot midthigh.

"Isn't it a bit short?" she asked wryly, tugging at the stretchy fabric.

Annie slapped her hands away.

"Nah. That's how it's supposed to look," Jessica said.

Even Val signed "beautiful"—a word Michelle had only learned that morning.

Michelle took a deep breath, held it for a moment, then shrugged, accepting the inevitable. Short of hurting their feelings, she wasn't going to get out of this house in anything other than what she had on, so she might as well enjoy it.

"I suppose I'm ready, then," she said as she slid her feet into a pair of delicate, high-heeled pumps, her stomach tightening in anticipation at how Devlin would react to her outfit. She could only hope he wouldn't laugh out loud.

He won't laugh, the little voice inside her head warned. And she knew it was true. He was in for a surprise once confronted with her sensual attire, but she knew he would be pleased. Very pleased. Therein lay another sort of danger.

"Here's your purse," Sammy said, offering Michelle a tiny beaded affair. "There's a comb, mirror and a five-dollar bill inside."

Michelle nearly chuckled aloud, recognizing her own words in that statement. How many times had she sent these girls out on their own dates with some money tucked inside their purses for emergencies?

"Make sure you keep a clear head," Annie warned.

"Don't give in to peer pressure," Marie added.

"No alcohol, no—"

"Sammy, Miss Worthington is an adult. Those rules don't apply," Annie reminded her friend.

Sammy appeared perplexed for an instant, then grinned. "Oh, yeah."

Michelle took the purse, looping the cord over her shoulder. "Thanks, guys. I really appreciate all the trouble you've gone to on my behalf."

It was Annie who leaned close to give her a quick hug. "You deserve it, Michelle. You've been the best thing that's ever happened to us."

The comment caused a lump to gather in Michelle's throat. She'd been in a bit of shock ever since Annie had told her about the prospective evening. But before she could say anything more, she was being pushed out of her bedroom and toward the staircase. Once at the top, the hands at her back disappeared and she found herself alone, staring down at the man waiting in the foyer.

Devlin's eyes glowed in the light being cast by the chandelier, his gaze raking her body with a thoroughness that caused her cheeks to pinken. He definitely liked what he saw—and the feeling was mutual. He was looking very dashing in a dark suit and white shirt with a hand-painted tie, and she was immediately glad that the girls had seen fit to improve upon her own wardrobe.

"Darling! You look divine."

Michelle's gaze skipped from her escort to the be-jeweled woman stepping into the foyer. Only Maude would feel it necessary to wear diamonds during a stint as chaperon.

"Hello, Mother. Do you have everything you need?"

The woman nodded, waving a small booklet above her head. "I've rented *Little Women* and *The Parent Trap* from the video store—although your little monsters did their best to persuade me to rent *Terminator II* and *Interview With the Vampire*. I conceded to their choices only as far as getting this Nintendo game. The boys are going to teach me how to play Mario 3.''

Michelle began to descend the staircase, her fingers trailing lightly over the banister railing. ''That should keep you busy.''

''My word, yes. We've got Chinese takeout for dinner, cheesecake for dessert, and popcorn for later.''

Michelle rolled her eyes, coming to a halt mere inches away from Devlin Rhett. Maybe it was the clothes she wore, but she could feel the heat from his body, the taut awareness he controlled just below his surface calm.

''The food choices are certainly...eclectic,'' she commented, scrambling for something to say. Anything to dispel the anticipation seeping through her veins like molten lava.

''We'll bring some antacid home with us just in case,'' Devlin said as he draped a wide lace scarf over Michelle's shoulders. Vaguely, Michelle noted that one of the girls must have brought him the wrap, then the thought skittered from her head as she absorbed the light pressure of his hands on her bare skin.

''Here, Mr. Rhett.'' Pete scampered into the vestibule, handing him a gaily colored coupon. ''This is your gift certificate.''

Rhett released Michelle to take the note, folding the paper and tucking it into his inside pocket.

"Thanks, Pete." He ruffled the boy's hair. "Maude, make sure you—"

"See to the alarm system. I know, I know."

Grinning, Devlin took Michelle's hand, linking their fingers together. "Don't wait up for us."

Michelle's cheeks grew hot at the parting comment, but thankfully, no one seemed to notice as Devlin led her outside to where the Rolls-Royce was parked and waiting.

He opened the passenger door. "After you."

She did her best to sink onto the seat in her most ladylike manner, but even then, she couldn't prevent the way her hem rose to a point midthigh.

Looking up, she managed to catch Devlin's eye. Although he didn't speak, an instant allure arced between them, filling the air with an electric awareness. In that instant, she knew that it was inevitable that he kiss her, touch her, caress her before the night was through.

"Are you sure you want to do this?" he murmured.

She knew he was giving her one last chance to escape, one last chance to avoid elevating their relationship to a much more personal plane.

When she spoke, her voice was but a thread of silk. "I'm sure."

THE HEATED SILENCE grew as they pulled away from Worthington and into the nighttime shadows. Michelle wrapped her shawl more securely over her bare shoulders and stared at the scenery flashing by her window, but the technique did little to dampen the buildup of desire thrumming between them. She could only hope that her kids hadn't chosen some secluded French restaurant with flickering candlelight and secluded tables. If they had, she was sunk.

She needn't have worried. She'd forgotten that even though her kids might be more mature than other adolescents their age, they were still kids. The Rolls-Royce eased to a stop near the neon-lit warehouse where the name of the establishment, Jumpin' Jack's, was strafed time and again with the beam of a huge spotlight. Rock music thumped through the open door and velvet cords held a line of bizarrely dressed customers at bay while a burly bouncer checked their identification.

Michelle's vision of a quiet, intimate dinner scattered like buckshot.

"How long do you think it will take to get in?" she asked, eyeing the queue of people stretching around the side of the building.

"Wait here."

Devlin parked the Rolls in the red zone by the front entrance and jumped out. Cutting to the head of the line, he bent toward the bouncer, conversing with him for several minutes. Then he was loping back to the car. Opening the passenger door, he ordered, "Keep your head down."

"What?"

"Keep your head down."

"We're in a red zone."

Devlin grinned. "I know."

Michelle wasn't sure why she was supposed to follow such an odd request, but she did so automatically as she was rushed to the front door and let into Jumpin' Jack's before she had time to think.

"What was all that about?" she shouted into the din of music, laughter and conversation.

"I told the bouncer you were a European princess intent on getting a taste of American nightlife."

Her jaw dropped and she had to remind herself to close it. "He went for it?"

"With that car, why wouldn't he? Especially if you gave the impression of being particularly camera shy."

She stared at him a moment longer, then began to laugh. Trust Devlin Rhett to know just what tale to spin.

"Come on."

He had taken her hand again and began to lead her through the crowd of onlookers toward the dance floor in the center of the refurbished warehouse.

"What are you doing?"

Michelle was sure that her voice had been more than loud enough for him to hear her, but he ignored the question, drawing her onto the hardwood floor.

Overhead, gaily colored lights swooped and flashed. The music surrounded them, the vibrations coming through the ground to be absorbed into their feet. Then Devlin was drawing her into his arms and moving to the beat.

Michelle sucked in her breath, her own fingers curling reflexively into his jacket. In the close quarters they'd been forced to adopt, her thigh had slipped between his. Her hips had been drawn close, her breasts pressed into his chest. And when he began to move, swaying back and forth to the slow ballad pouring from the speakers, she discovered that there was nothing more intimate, more erotic, than being trapped in the middle of a crowded nightclub.

Toni Braxton was crooning over the loudspeakers and Michelle surrendered to the singer's breathless tone, which stirred up sensual images intensified by Devlin's touch.

When Devlin leaned down, his lips grazing her cheek, she sighed against him, her hands locking at the back of his neck.

"Kiss me," she whispered.

He couldn't possibly have heard her, but he didn't need to. She was sure he could see what she wanted, needed.

His lips brushed against hers, the gesture so fleeting and real that it was torture when he drew back to look at her.

"Do you know what you're doing to me?" she could see him saying.

"Yes." Her grip grew more insistent, forcing him to bend closer, closer. "Yes. I'm playing with fire, and I like it."

Then she was kissing him, her tongue slipping into his mouth to begin an erotic chase.

He tasted so good, felt so good, it was impossible for her to get enough of him. But that didn't stop her from trying. She flattened her body to his as he continued to move to the music, his hips thrusting, his body twisting and dipping so that she had no recourse but to hold him as tightly as possible and absorb the sensations rocking her to the very core.

Never before had she experienced a passion so overwhelming, so mind-consuming. The sensations raced through her body like white lightning, obliterating her inhibitions and exposing her for what she was—a woman who longed to be needed.

When Devlin broke free, gasping for breath, she read in his expression the same yearnings that must be etched on her own.

"Let's get out of here," he rasped.

She could only nod.

This time, he held her close to his side as he navigated the sea of people. As soon as they burst outside, he dug into his pocket, removing a folded bill and holding it out in the direction of the bouncer.

"Thanks," he said.

The bouncer stared at him in disbelief. "You were only in there a few minutes."

"Like I said, she only wanted a taste of American nightlife," Devlin said, and Michelle giggled, doing her best to keep her head averted.

Devlin opened the driver's side and she slid to the center of the seat. When he followed, revving the engine, she wrapped her hand around his thigh, causing him to hiss. She liked that sound, liked the power it gave her, the surge of pleasure.

"Where are you taking me?" she asked as the Rolls shot down the street at a speed that seemed at odds with the sedate luxury car.

"My place." He glanced at her. "Any objections?"

"None at all."

He pulled the car into an underground parking lot beneath a high-rise building. After shutting off the engine, he drew her toward the elevator. As soon as the doors had closed, he pulled her into his arms, his head swooping down for a passionate kiss.

Then there was no more time for words. Michelle arched against him, knowing that nothing in her life had ever felt so right or so real.

She barely noticed as the doors slid open and Devlin backed her into the hall, fumbling with his keys while he strung vibrant kisses down the arch of her throat. Then she was being swept into his arms and he was striding into his apartment, kicking the door closed behind him.

She had a vague impression of black leather and stark photographs before he was taking her into his bedroom and dropping her into the center of an immense four-poster bed.

"Do you want me to stop?" he whispered against her as he stripped off his jacket.

"No." She was tugging at his tie.

"You're sure?"

"Perfectly sure."

In no time at all, their clothing was strewn across the floor.

Michelle gasped the first time she saw him completely naked. Kneeling in the center of the bed, she drew him to her, her hands lovingly stroking the muscles of his chest and abdomen, then lower to the ridges and planes she had studied while he'd repaired the roof.

"You're beautiful," she whispered.

"Not as beautiful as you," he responded, lowering her to the bed and framing her face in his hands. "I've never met anyone like you, Michelle. I want you to know that."

She nodded, touched profoundly by his words.

"And I'll take care of you. I promise."

He slid open his nightstand drawer, withdrawing a small foil packet. Michelle was secretly touched that he had taken the precaution without her asking.

"Love me, Devlin," she said, sliding her hands beneath his arms and pulling him on top of her. His weight was more arousing than she would have thought possible. He was so taut and warm.

The thinking part was over, there was only time to feel. She immersed herself in the sensations he inspired with his hands, his lips, his body. He worshiped her, body and soul, until she could no longer wait. Drawing him closer, ever closer, she pleaded with him in hoarse whispers until finally he readied himself, looked deep into her eyes, and plunged into the core of her.

She sucked in her breath in delight, her head arching back and her eyes closing as he filled her completely. Then she was clutching at him as he began to move, to rock, to drive into the very heart of her. A shimmering tension gathered deep in her body, and soon it was impossible to think of anything but this man, this moment, this incredible experience. She could feel the pinnacle approaching and she surrendered herself to it completely, crying out when her body imploded and shuddered with its release.

Vaguely, she felt Devlin's body follow suit, the trembling of his shoulders, the guttural moan that rent from his throat. Then he was arching against her, reveling in his own climax.

Reality returned to Michelle slowly and sweetly, like a velvet sunrise. Bit by bit, she became aware of Devlin's head in the crook of her shoulder and his legs sprawled between her own.

Summoning what little energy she had left, she brushed the tangled hair from his forehead. His lashes flickered and he looked at her, the expression in his eyes so intense, so wonderful, that for one fleeting moment, she thought it might be love.

But then he was rolling away, drawing her into the crook of his arm and pressing her head onto his shoulder.

"Devlin?" she began, wanting to know if what she'd seen was true.

"Shh, sweetheart," he murmured, stroking her hair with his palm. "We've got all the time in the world to sort things out."

His words stunned her, both for the casual endearment and the content behind his pronouncement.

We've got all the time in the world to sort things out.

Closing her eyes, she allowed herself to succumb to the exhaustion permeating her body. They would talk later.

They had all the time in the world.

"SO TELL ME MORE about yourself, Devlin Rhett," Michelle demanded.

Devlin propped his spine against the headboard, studying the woman who sat cross-legged in the middle of his bed, wearing nothing more than one of his T-shirts.

Both of them had slept for about an hour, then, awakened by their hunger, Devlin had called a local bistro and arranged delivery of thick croissant sandwiches, a selection of sliced fresh fruits, and a bottle of wine.

"What do you want to know?"

"Everything."

She was breaking pieces of her sandwich off, tipping her head back, and dropping the food into her mouth. With her disheveled hair and too large shirt, she looked adorable. Completely and utterly adorable.

"You already know about Mum and Dad and Ross."

"But I know nothing about the way you were raised."

He paused to think as he chewed a bite of his food, wondering how much he should tell her. But even as caution raised its head, he discovered that he wanted her to know as much as possible.

"Life was pretty normal until my parents divorced, then I lived a six month split."

"Six month split?"

"Half the year with Mum in England, half with my father in Tennessee."

"So your mother returned to Britain?"

He nodded. "My brother was in a special boarding school and she found she was happier near her own family."

"Did you resent the arrangement? Being moved from parent to parent?"

"Not really. By that time I was a teen myself and not much different than the kids at Worthington. I was brash and rebellious and full of my own importance."

She grinned. "Meaning you were trouble with a capital *T*."

He chuckled. "Exactly. But through some miracle, my parents managed to persuade me to graduate high school."

"How did they do that?"

"Bribery."

"What did they bribe you with?"

"A car."

She took a quick sip of her wine. "What kind?"

"Porsche."

Michelle choked and he patted her back.

"That's some kind of bribery," she sputtered when she could finally speak.

"I still have it in storage. Mint condition, only a thousand miles."

"How did that happen? I would have thought that you would have driven it to death."

"I probably would have done if I hadn't joined the army."

She choked again, and he took the paper cup from her hand, putting it on the nightstand. "Maybe you should dispense with imbibing until I finish answering your questions."

Michelle was thumping her chest to get control of her coughing fit. When she finally regained her breath, she regarded him with sparkling eyes.

"You joined the army?"

"Yes."

"Which one?"

"Ours."

He saw the way her eyes widened at that response and he supposed that with his accent she'd always considered him more British than American.

"They must have found you an unusual soldier, what with the way you talked."

"I suppose."

"So, how did you get from the army to butlering?"

The question caused him to stop and think. He wasn't a butler, and this woman needed to know that. She'd given him her trust and her passion. He should see to it that she knew the truth before she could give him her heart.

Her heart? Was that what he wanted?

Yes. Oh, yes. He leaned forward, taking her hands. "Michelle, there's something you need to know."

The phone rang and he ignored it.

"I haven't been entirely—"

Ring.

"—forthcoming."

Ring.

Michelle lunged across the bed and grabbed the receiver. "You'd better answer this first."

Inwardly swearing, he held the receiver to his ear. "Yeah," he barked.

"Mr. Rhett?"

He frowned, hearing a shrill *whoop-whoop* in the background. "Who's this?"

"It's Pete. Mrs. Worthington told me to call you at this number. The alarm's gone off and she says you have to come home."

Before Rhett could question him further, the line clicked and went dead. From somewhere under his clothes, his pager began an insistent *beep, beep, beep.*

"What's wrong?" Michelle breathed when Devlin slowly replaced the receiver.

"It's the kids," he said, already jumping from the bed and reaching for their clothes. "We've got to get home."

Chapter Twelve

They arrived back at Worthington amid a swirl of police lights and the cacophony of a dozen teenagers
trying to talk at once. Even Burt Escalson, the new
arrival, was pacing back and forth and swearing at the
effrontery of the would-be assailant, while Sammy
kept track of the epithets for the cuss jar.

Michelle immediately went to the teens while Devlin strode toward one of the familiar faces next to the
first patrol car.

"What's up, Vic?" he asked, carefully keeping his
back to the group on the porch so that they wouldn't
be able to read his expression—or worse yet, that Val
wouldn't read his lips.

Vic Patrillo had been the officer on call the first
night Michelle had summoned 911, and he grimaced.
"What a mess." He gestured to a pair of boys in the
back of the squad car. "These two are friends of Elliot Grover."

"Damn."

"Don't worry, I doubt he's involved in all this. I think they were worried about their buddy and decided to take matters into their own hands. They waited until most of your group there was positioned in the front of the house, then, since the alarm hadn't been turned on yet, they sneaked into the back and hid in the basement. According to their statements, they just wanted to take Valerie to meet with her boyfriend. They waited until dark, crept up the stairs, and tried to get into her room."

With each word, a horrible sense of guilt rose in Devlin's chest. He should have been here. He never should have forgotten that he had been sent here to protect these kids.

These kids? his conscience echoed, and he found himself turning to watch the huddle of adolescents crowding around Michelle, all of them trying to talk to her at once.

Somewhere in the background, Vic continued. "They made a mistake and woke Annie instead of Val—although how they could mistake the identity of a kid nine months pregnant, I'll never know. Anyway, all hell broke loose. Annie started screaming, Val was beating at them with a book. The boys rushed in, Willie with his baseball bat. Awakened by the noise, some elderly gentleman named Wilson purposely set off the alarm, and that woman over there in the pink ran into the bedroom and began tying up the assailants with the phone cord she'd ripped out of her wall."

Devlin could see it all in his head and he was amazed when his throat tightened with emotion. "Was anybody hurt?"

Vic chortled, gesturing to the two teenagers in the patrol car. "These two have got some bumps and bruises, but I think they'll survive. I'm afraid we're going to have to take them downtown."

"Fine."

Devlin didn't bother to offer any goodbyes, knowing he'd be seeing Vic in short order at the station, as soon as he could determine if and how Michelle intended to press charges. Instead, his attention latched on to Maude Worthington.

As he he walked toward her, he was sure that she knew what he meant to say because she stiffened.

"We need to talk, Maude."

She glanced at the kids, the police, then her daughter.

"Tonight. I'll meet you by the pool when all the furor dies down," she said.

Then, not bothering to give him the chance to argue, she escaped inside.

IT WAS PAST MIDNIGHT before Devlin felt that it was safe for him to meet with Michelle's mother.

His body throbbed with a weariness that went beyond being merely physical and as the cool air lapped over his body, he realized that it had been several hours since he and Michelle had made love. Several excruciating hours of being tormented by what-ifs. What if Michelle found out about the subterfuge he'd employed before he could tell her? What if Maude wouldn't release him from his current job?

The stress and worry had taken its toll on his body and he was forced to admit that he wasn't as adept at handling the anxieties as he'd once been. Moreover, he no longer found it a thrill to live on the edge. As he walked down the flagstone path, he discovered that he longed to settle down—and the thought didn't scare him as much as it might have a mere decade ago. He wasn't going soft, he realized. But his priorities *had* changed dramatically.

Devlin was relieved to see that Maude was waiting for him. She'd stretched out on a padded chaise. Her eyes were closed, but he knew she wasn't asleep.

"So, Devlin?" she asked as he approached. "What do you think of my daughter?"

He didn't answer, stopping only a few scant feet away.

Her eyes flicked open and she smiled knowingly. "That must have been some date."

Devlin remained silent, still, hoping that he appeared as stern as he intended.

"I want out of our bargain, Maude."

"My, my, you sound so dangerous," she purred. Lifting her hands over her head, she stretched like a cat, then rose from her chair with such infinite grace, he was reminded that this woman had spent her life on the stage.

"Wilson?"

On cue, Wilson emerged from the shadows carrying a silver tray that held a glass of chilled wine, a bottle of beer, and a vellum envelope.

"A drink, Devlin, dear?"

He started to shake his head, but she pouted and took the bottle by the neck, extending it in his direction. "After all, I think we should toast each other for a job well done."

One of his brows lifted inquisitively as he automatically took the bottle.

"I received notification from my husband that the brigand responsible for the threats has been apprehended." She gestured to the thick envelope from the tray. "Your services are no longer needed, my sweet." Her pansy blue eyes twinkled. "At least not as a butler."

He stared at the envelope for some time, knowing that it held his pay and probably an exorbitant tip.

"Keep it."

She paused, her glass of wine held midway to her lips. "I beg your pardon?"

"I want you to add what you have there to the tutoring clinic you already promised to organize for these kids."

Maude didn't speak, but her gaze remained intense.

"You weren't thinking of backing out on the agreement, were you, Maude?"

"No. I don't suppose I was." She flashed him a smile. "But it's cheeky of you to remind me of my obligations all the same."

She drained the wineglass and set it on the tray. "I'll have Wilson contact my lawyers to make the arrangements."

"Thank you."

Maude gestured for Wilson to precede her into the house. But before she passed Devlin, Maude paused, cupping his face in one hand.

"I think the two of you will be quite happy."

Devlin thought of denying her statement. After all, he wasn't sure what he intended to do himself yet. His emotions were so new, so tenuous, so uncertain, that he hadn't planned much beyond telling Michelle the truth.

Maude chuckled softly, patting his cheek. "Just remember...if she's angry at first, give her time to cool off. My daughter might be stubborn, but she isn't stupid."

Then, still laughing to herself, she disappeared inside the house.

For some time, Devlin stood in the darkness, drinking his beer, rehearsing just what he would do, what he would say. He had no doubt that Michelle would be angry at him for his pretense of being her butler. He was even more sure that she would be furious when she discovered he'd been trying to protect her.

So how was he going to explain it all?

Sighing, he tossed the empty bottle in the trash and rolled his shoulders in an effort to release the tension that had gathered there, but the action had little effect. Gazing down at the surface of the pool shimmering in the moonlight, he had the sudden urge to immerse himself in the silky depths, to clear his head and cool his body. As Michelle had requested, he'd fixed the filter some time ago, but he hadn't yet replaced the underwater lighting. No one would know if he took a quick swim.

Stripping to his briefs, he dove into the deep end, his body tensing at the shock of the much cooler water. But when he surfaced and breathed deeply, he felt better than he had in hours. Maybe after a few laps his head would clear and he'd be able to think.

Heading toward the opposite end of the pool, he struck cleanly through the water, his arms and legs straining for speed until he could flip, turn, and begin striving for the opposite end.

Over and over he swam laps until his muscles began to tremble and his breath to hitch. Midway, he stopped, sank beneath the surface, and bobbed up again, delighting in the cool air that caressed his wet hair.

"That's quite a workout for the middle of the night."

The voice shot to the very heart of him and Devlin looked up to discover that sometime during his swim, Michelle had come to join him. She'd dipped her legs into the shallow end by the stairs and was making idle circles with her toes.

"What inspired such a burst of energy?"

Devlin couldn't have stayed still had a gun been put to his head. Employing a lazy breaststroke, he began to move toward her.

"After our break-in, I thought I should come outside and check on a few things."

"Oh really," she drawled. "I thought I heard my mother's voice at one point."

"I'm sure you did. We had a brief talk."

"That must have been interesting."

She tugged at the tie of her cover-up and Devlin found that he couldn't speak, didn't want to speak. He was entranced by the way she pulled the satin belt free with all the expertise of a stripper.

"Did you find anything out of place when you looked around?"

Devlin shook his head. "No, nothing." His throat was dry and tight, his voice emerging with sandpaper roughness.

She didn't speak right away, and as the seconds ticked by, the placket of her robe parted more and more, revealing the dark, skimpy bikini she wore underneath.

"Miss Worthington," he chided, trying to appear shocked, but even to his own ears, he sounded much too pleased. "What in the world are you wearing?"

"Mr. Rhett, I think that I've allowed you to harbor some misconceptions."

Her wrap fell to the ground and moonlight teased her shoulders, her breasts, the swell of her hips. The water around him didn't feel nearly as cool as it had only seconds before.

"Oh, really?" he croaked.

"Mmm. I've been getting the impression that you think I'm a responsible grown-up through and through." She lowered herself into the pool, step by step. "Nothing could be further from the truth."

She slid through the water toward him, her body sleek and wet. Twining her arms around his neck, she kissed him with the fervor of youth and desire—and for the first time since coming to Worthington, Devlin found himself responding wholeheartedly. He was finally free to love her.

Love?

Yes, love. He loved this woman body and soul. All that remained was to tell her.

Their embrace grew heated and intense, the water adding to the sensations building between them. Devlin's mouth and fingers were greedy, seeking the sensitive points of her body that caused her to gasp. But he was not alone in his exploration. She, too, was eagerly blazing a sensual path over his shoulders and down his spine.

Knowing things were progressing quickly—too quickly—Devlin jerked free of her kiss. When she mewled in distress, he pressed quick kisses down her neck.

"I want to enjoy you," he whispered. "This is all going too swiftly."

His statement caused her to relax again and grow sinuous in his arms, but when she shivered, he asked, "Do you want to go in?"

She shook her head. "Wilson and Frieda are necking on the couch."

He chuckled. "Shouldn't you be chaperoning?"

Michelle grinned. "Until I'm given legal custody of those two, it's none of my business."

He took the weight of her body, lifting her, carrying her to one of the chaises. Then, he stretched his body over hers, warming her with the heat of his own skin. His hands cupped her shoulders, moving inward so that his thumb could stroke the hollow at the base of her throat. But such small caresses led to more and more, until he was unable to endure the exquisite agony any longer.

Hungrily, he began kissing her, loving her, adoring her with his lips in the way that he didn't feel he could ever do with words.

She made soft gasping sounds, clutching at his hair. But she didn't draw away from him. Instead, she held him close, trembling against him.

"I want you, Michelle," he whispered against her.

"I know."

"But we shouldn't do this here."

"I know."

"It could lead to so many complications."

"Uh-huh."

"But I can't stop. Please don't make me stop."

He took her silence as tacit acceptance and leaned into her, delighting in the way her breasts brushed against his chest and her legs parted to allow one of his thighs to lie between them. He gasped when her hips arched, bringing her body tightly against his arousal.

"We've got to get out of here," she gasped.

"I know, but I can't stop."

She laid her fingers against his lips, forcing him to draw back and look at her, really look at her—at the heady excitement to be found in her eyes and the flush of her cheeks.

"You don't have to stop. You only have to wait."

With that, she pushed him away, rising to her feet.

"Come on, Butler Rhett. I think it's time we headed inside."

"What about Wilson and Frieda?"

"We'll go in the back door."

They made no sound as they entered the house. When he would have led the way to his own bedroom, she shook her head.

"My place," she murmured. "We'll take the back staircase."

"I haven't fixed one of the treads yet."

"So we'll step over that one."

Tiptoeing, he followed her upstairs, and from there to the center doors.

"Won't someone be able to hear us up here?"

She shook her head. "My grandmother was especially fond of the "bedroom tango" as she put it. When the house was remodeled, she insisted that the walls be made double thick. That's why it's such a great place to keep teenagers."

Opening the door, she whispered, "Be prepared."

"For what?" He was still trying to get over the information that her grandmother had indulged in the "bedroom tango" and hadn't been shy about informing her granddaughter of such a thing.

"I've kept the room pretty much as she left it."

His brows rose. "Curiouser and curiouser."

But as soon as he stepped inside and she switched on the lights, he knew why he'd been warned.

Her grandmother had indeed lived in the heart of the Art Deco period. Gilded, rose-colored lamps were shaded in silk and fringe and draped with floral scarves. A bold geometric design had been embroidered on the ebony carpet, and the scheme was con-

tinued on the walls in blocks of black, silver and pink.
A huge vanity table was laden with cut-glass perfume
decanters and a gold-plated toiletry set. A group of
framed prints revealed that Michelle's grandmother
had a fondness for some of Erte's and Maxfield Par-
rish's more scandalous renderings, as well as several
prints from the *Kama Sutra*.

He whistled under his breath.

"If you think that's something..." She let the
phrase trail away as she flipped another switch. Lights
against the far wall sprang on, revealing a bed—not
just a bed, but a pasha's paradise.

The headboard had been made of starburst-shaped
panels of beveled mirror and gleaming mahogany. Silk
scarves in shades of pink, russet and black had been
looped over the mahogany canopy posts and fell to the
floor to puddle on the dark carpet.

"It's incredible," he murmured, wondering if he
would be able to live up to the promise of this room.
He should be dressed in the billowing robes of a sheikh
or a sharply pressed tuxedo.

"I'll be right back."

She left him alone, making her way to what he assumed was an adjoining bathroom. As the door
closed, he wondered what she was doing. Moreover,
he wondered what *he* was supposed to do. He suddenly understood how a bridegroom must feel waiting
for his beloved to emerge from the lavatory.

His *beloved?*

What in the world had possessed him to think such a thing? *Beloved?* It wasn't even a term he was accustomed to using. It was completely antiquated, completely...

In keeping with this room.

In keeping with a man contemplating marriage.

The thought was enough to cool his ardor. Marriage. His first marriage had been a disaster, how could he even be thinking such a thing in connection with Michelle Worthington?

But even as the doubts swirled inside him, a feeling that was far more powerful and intense pushed them away. Love. He loved Michelle Worthington. In doing so, he wanted her for all time, not just a few nights or a few months. He wanted to grow old with her. He wanted to be a part of her life, a part of her dreams.

MICHELLE LEANED BACK against the bathroom door, smiling softly to herself. Desire still slid through her veins, insistent and warm.

She knew she should pause to think about the consequences of what she was about to do, but she was so tired of thinking, so tired of planning. She just wanted to drown in sensual seas for an evening.

But first, a shower to wash away the chlorine....

She twisted the knobs to the ornately tiled cubicle and stepped inside, lifting her face to the spray. Once she'd washed, she would see about finding something slinky to wear.

But when Michelle heard the click of the latch, all thoughts of lingerie scattered. Every nerve in her body quivered to attention as the shower door squeaked open, then closed.

"Mind if I join you?" Devlin asked behind her, his voice dark and deep and infinitely arousing.

"No. I don't mind."

Then she was turning in his arms, her mouth seeking his.

What had begun in the pool quickly ignited anew. But this time, there was the added dimension of being totally unclothed and ensconced in complete privacy.

The last of Michelle's inhibitions washed away with the chlorine and she willingly gave herself up to the ecstasy this man inspired, knowing that what happened this evening would be different. After the passion had been appeased, they would talk and decide where this relationship was heading. Until then, she would revel in Devlin's embrace, in the power of his kisses, in the depth of his adoration.

Because she loved him, like no other.

He reached behind her, shutting off the water, and Michelle didn't protest. Nor did she protest when he scooped her into his arms and carried her to the bed.

Tonight would be but the prelude to something even more special. She knew that.

Heart and soul.

Chapter Thirteen

"Mi-chelle!"

The deep, booming voice came from the lower hall, startling Michelle from her slumber. Sitting up in bed, she gradually became aware of her surroundings and scooped the covers against her naked breasts.

Looking down, she gazed at the man who lay on his stomach, his arms cupped around the pillows, a lock of hair falling over his forehead.

"Michelle!"

It took the second cry for Michelle to realize who was shouting at her.

"Daddy?" she whispered incredulously, her limbs growing weak. The sensation was not a new one. It was the same reaction she'd had to that man since childhood.

In an instant, she saw this room as he would see it— the rumpled sheets, the man stretched out beside her, their nude bodies. She threw the covers back, leapt from the bed and scrambled toward her closet. Somehow, she managed to slip into her underthings and tug a loose, cotton dress over her head.

As she dashed to the door, she had a quick glimpse of her hair. It was more than obvious how she'd spent the last few hours.

"Blast," she muttered under her breath, running to the dressing table and running a brush through the tangles.

"Mi-chhellle!"

She threw the silver-back brush down, her heart thudding in alarm. Judging by the proximity of his shouts, her father was making his way up the stairs.

She stepped out of the room just as Gerald Worthington reached the upper corridor.

"Daddy!"

Her father was a huge, barrel-chested man with a florid face that had been made even redder by his heightened emotions.

"What the hell is going on?" he bellowed, shaking a finger in the air.

Maude stepped out of her own bedroom at that moment, belting the sash to her jacquard dressing gown. Michelle couldn't account for the mixture of guilt and dread that spread over her mother's features.

"Gerald! What are you doing here?"

"What am *I* doing here? What am *I* doing here? Dammit, what are you up to, Maude?"

Maude assumed a blank stare, even though it was obvious to everyone present that her brain was scrambling for a logical reply.

Unfortunately, in the absence of an explanation, Gerald turned to his daughter. "Do you know what your mother has been doing, young lady?"

Michelle shook her head in confusion, cringing when her bedroom door squeaked and she heard Devlin pad toward them.

"Michelle? What's going on out here? Why didn't you wake me?"

Gerald stiffened and stared. "Just who are you?"

The silence in the hall was so thick, Michelle feared it would smother her. All eyes turned in her direction as if her explanation would be considered some sort of test and she was the only person who would be given the opportunity to answer.

"Daddy, this is my... butler."

She cringed at the disappointment she found in Devlin's eyes. They'd never had a chance for the talk she'd anticipated. After making love, the two of them had drifted into an exhausted sleep. She regretted that fact now. If they'd only had a few minutes this morning, she could have explained her feelings. Then she could have felt comfortable introducing him as so much more than a mere employee.

"What's he doing in your bedroom?" her father demanded.

She winced, her attention drawn to Devlin's feet which were bare. It was only a matter of seconds before her father demanded clarification of that too, she was sure.

Michelle's assumption was correct. Gerald's eyes dipped and his mouth pursed. Then he glared at Devlin—who was wearing little more than a sheet—as if he were responsible for all the world's ills.

"You must be Maude's stooge."

Michelle's brow furrowed as her mother gasped and grasped him by the elbow.

"Gerald, Gerald!" she said, laughing uneasily. "I haven't seen you in ages. Why don't you take me out for coffee and we'll talk?"

Such a reaction was so unlike her mother that Michelle felt the first twinges of alarm.

Gerald shook free of his ex-wife's pink-lacquered nails.

"Maude, I want an explanation, and I want it now!"

"I'll be happy to give you anything you want, Gerald, just—"

"Mother, what have you done?"

All eyes zeroed in on Michelle and she folded her arms in an attempt to still the twinges of anxiety settling somewhere in the region of her heart.

Maude flashed her a wide smile. "I don't know what you mean."

"Dammit, Maude, don't play the innocent," Gerald growled. "You were never any good at it."

Maude glared at him.

"Tell her. And tell *me.*" Gerald reached into his jacket, withdrawing a folded piece of paper. "I want to know why you've concocted some preposterous story about threats being made against Michelle."

"What?" Michelle gasped, looking at her mother, father, then Devlin. It was Devlin's expression that held her attention. He was staring at Maude as if she'd suddenly grown a second head.

"Gerald, I—"

"Maude, out with it. What's all this nonsense about someone making death threats against my family to ensure a diplomatic trade agreement?"

Michelle's jaw dropped.

Devlin's hands balled into fists.

Maude flushed, offering another small laugh, but the sound was hollow. "I . . ."

Michelle felt the ice flowing through her veins, bit by bit, muscle by muscle.

Death threats?

"Really, Gerald. If you'd just let me get my wits about me." She offered a gay tinkle of laughter. "Michelle wasn't ever in any harm."

"She wasn't ever in any harm?" This time it was Devlin who repeated the words.

"Devlin! You know what I mean. She wasn't ever in any *real* harm. What I mean to say is..." Maude bit her lip and gripped her hands together. "I only wanted the two of you to meet."

The twinges in Michelle's chest were growing into a solid ache.

"Mother, what are you trying to say?"

The hall thrummed with tension before her mother offered a half sob and said, "I made up a little story about your being in danger. After meeting Devlin, I knew he'd be perfect for you... perfect! But you wouldn't listen to me if I said such a thing. You were convinced I was always interfering in your life—not that it's true, mind you. I never interfere. I just... meddle sometimes."

"Dammit, Maude," Devlin rasped.

"I'm sorry, darling. I know you're probably angry with me, too, but you were so busy all the time. I knew you wouldn't take time out of your schedule for some matchmaking, so I invented the story about the death threats and hired you to be Michelle's bodyguard."

"My *bodyguard?*"

Maude had the grace to appear shamefaced. "Then Wilson and I arranged a few accidents—"

"It was *you* who threw the brick through the window?"

She nodded.

"Brick, what brick?" Michelle asked, but at her mother's guilty expression, she suddenly knew. "You broke our kitchen window with a *brick?* Peggy was sent to the hospital after that stunt."

"I know, dear, and I'm frightfully sorry. We thought she'd already left the room. I never would have allowed one of your kids to be hurt. If I'd known someone was there, we would have thought of something else."

"Dammit, Mother, how could you be so irresponsible?"

Maude's eyes filled with tears. "I wanted you to be happy."

"What made you think I wasn't happy?"

"How could you have been? You were all alone."

"Happiness isn't contingent upon a relationship, Mother."

"Come now, dear. Haven't you been ever so much more content with a man around the place?"

Content? The word didn't even begin to describe the gamut of emotions that Michelle had experienced since Devlin's arrival.

"I knew you would be beside yourself if you found a special someone, Michelle, and I knew Devlin was that man. I had to do something. I didn't want you to spend your days alone like me."

"What did you hope to accomplish by sending him here under false pretenses?"

"I knew the two of you would get along. I felt it in my bones. Once you had grown to care for him, I knew you would forgive both of us for the slight fib."

Michelle fought to control her temper, failed, and whirled to confront Devlin. "What have you got to say about all this?"

"I had no idea your mother had—"

"No idea?"

"No," he said emphatically. "I thought I'd been sent here to protect you."

But that information was like a match to dried timber.

"And if that was the case, why didn't you inform me of your reasons for being here?"

"Your mother thought—"

"I don't care what my mother thought." She took a deep breath, but even that couldn't blunt her anger. "How dare you? How *dare* you? I have been put in charge of these kids, I've sworn to help them, protect them. Yet, you and my mother waltz into this institution uninvited, without so much as a thought as to how this could affect us all. What if the Foundation got wind of this nonsense? Or the parents of some of these kids? Or their caseworkers? How dare you take everything so lightly, then beg off taking responsibility for your actions by telling me there was never any real danger? That this was all some elaborate prank?"

"Michelle," he murmured placatingly, taking her elbow.

"No!" She wrenched free. "I don't want to hear any more. I don't want to see any more." She gave them all a heated glare. "I want the whole lot of you out of this house within the hour. If you aren't gone by then, I'll have every one of you arrested for trespassing.''

Spinning on her toe, she raced to the staircase, knowing that she had to get away from them before she began to cry. They mustn't see how much they'd hurt her, how much they'd shaken her faith in them all.

SHE SPENT THE TIME away from the house in the garden, purposely staying there until more than an hour had passed and she heard the Rolls purr out of the drive. Only then did she wilt, succumbing to the tears which had lodged in her throat.

"Damn," she whispered miserably, making her way back to the house. "Damn them all. Damn them all for..."

For what?

For meddling?

For wanting her to be happy?

For wanting her to be safe?

She cursed again, letting herself into the kitchen, then stopping short when she found her father seated at the kitchen table.

"Daddy?" She quickly swiped at the tears. She should have known that Gerald Worthington had stayed for the last word.

He gestured to a chair. "Sit down, little one."

Since she was too overwrought to argue, she did as she was told.

Her father poured her a cup of coffee and placed it in front of her. Then, after retrieving one for himself, he resumed his own seat.

"I spoke to your mother."

Michelle opened her mouth, prepared to utter some defensive reply, but as the words sank into her brain, she realized he hadn't said anything that would require a retort on her part.

"What she did was unforgivable and entirely... brazen."

Michelle's jaw dropped when her father's chest rumbled in the beginnings of a laugh.

"I suppose that's why I've missed her so much these last few years."

"Missed her?" she echoed.

He clasped her hand, squeezing it in encouragement. "Your mother is one of a kind, Michelle. She's talented, exotic and overbearing. For a while, I convinced myself that the bad overwhelmed the good. But when I saw her today, all filled with self-righteous vitality because she'd been trying to manipulate our little girl's happiness, I was thunderstruck. In a flash, I saw where my life was headed. How I was destined to be all alone if I didn't learn to prioritize. Suddenly, I was ashamed of the way I ignored your mother and you while you were small. I should have been there for you. Will you forgive me, baby?"

The plea for forgiveness was so unexpected, the tears returned again, spilling over her lashes. "Oh, Daddy." She sighed, leaning into his open arms.

His broad hands held her close, patting her back, soothing her as her frustration melted away in a fit of weeping. When at long last she grew calmer, he framed her face, forcing her to look at him.

"Don't be too harsh on your mother," he urged. "Tell her you forgive her. And as for that young man..." He touched her chin. "Just remember that she lied to him, too."

"But, Daddy, he—"

"Do you love him?"

She nodded.

"Then forget about the rest. I'm here to tell you that pride can be an awfully cold bed partner."

"But I told him to go away." Her stomach clenched. "I don't know how to get ahold of him. I don't have a phone number or an address. He took me to his apartment once, but I wasn't paying attention to how we got there." She choked on a fresh sob. "Daddy, what am I going to do?"

"Michelle? Michelle!"

The call came from deep in the house. Again, she swiped away the tears, attempting to school her voice into something close to its usual timbre. "I'm in the kitchen, Sammy."

The girl burst through the door, her cheeks flushed.

"Hurry quick! Val's gone into labor."

Michelle stood. "Calm down. It's her first baby. It will be some time before we need to go to the hospital."

Sammy shook her head. "No, you don't understand. She's been in labor since last night, but she didn't want to worry anyone in case it was a false alarm. But the contractions are only a few minutes apart now and her water has broken."

Michelle was immediately spurred into action. Taking the keys to the van from the Peg-Board, she tossed them in her father's direction. "Can you get the car going?"

He was already on his way out the door.

"Sammy, get me some blankets and Val's suitcase."

Sammy hurried to do as she was told, rushing up the staircase. The noise alerted Jason and Rusty, who were just coming down.

"What's going on?" Rusty asked.

"Val's in labor. I've got to call the doctor."

As Michelle scrambled to dial the number of the doctor, then the hospital, then Val's parents, the house erupted in a flurry of activity. Sammy ran out to the van with the suitcase, Pete hard on her heels with some blankets and a pillow. Upstairs, doors slammed and footsteps pounded.

Michelle had just hung up the receiver from her final call when she heard Manuel shouting, "Out of his way, out of his way!" Looking up, she found Jason carrying Val in his arms. She was crying and gripping her belly, one of her hands forming Devlin's name.

"He isn't here right now," Michelle said when she caught the girl's eye. "But I'll send someone to get him, I promise."

Michelle hoped that Val had been able to read her lips before she was hit with another contraction and her eyes squeezed closed.

"You guys stay here and—"

"Stay here?" Willie interrupted. "We're not staying here. She's going to have a baby!"

Knowing that time was of the essence, Michelle didn't bother to argue. Climbing into the waiting van, she supervised the kids as they took their own positions, leaving one full bench for Val to lie upon.

"All right, Dad. Let's go."

The old van squealed as they raced out of the driveway and into the street. Michelle grasped Val's hand, wishing that there was some way of getting in touch with Devlin. She needed him. Val needed him. He was the one who had practiced to be the birthing coach, not Michelle—and she was feeling doubly inadequate at her inability to sign.

"How much farther?" she asked without looking up as Val gripped her hand.

"We're almost there."

Within seconds, the van was screeching to a halt and Willie was jumping from the front seat.

"Hey! We need a doctor out here! We're going to have a baby!"

Jason slid the side door open and lifted Val free of the van. By that time, a pair of nurses were rushing out of the door, one of them pushing a wheelchair.

"Come on, come on, get the lead out!" Kirk urged. "She's gonna have this kid on the sidewalk if you don't hurry."

Since Val was still clutching her hand, Michelle was forced to follow her up to Maternity. Before she really knew what was happening, she had been dressed in scrubs and surgical booties and was being drawn into the delivery room.

"But I've never practiced with her," she objected.

"She needs someone familiar," a nurse was saying. "Since she's deaf, she'll need all our help until we can get an interpreter."

Michelle's stomach was doing flip-flops. Her body was already beginning to shake. If she'd thought watching her kids have stitches was beyond her tolerance level, how much worse was this going to be?

Numbly, she took her place at Val's side. Again, the girl signed Devlin's name.

"I don't know where he is," Michelle whispered, knowing she must tell Val the truth. "I don't know if he'll get here in—"

"Miss Worthington, there's a Devlin Rhett out in the hall. He claims to be Val's interpreter."

Her heart crashed against her ribs in joy. "Yes. Yes! Send him in."

Within seconds, Devlin burst through the door, his body swathed in surgical green.

A sound that was half sob, half laugh escaped from Michelle's lips.

"How?" It was the only word she could manage to force out of her throat.

"Jason called my pager."

"Your pager?" she echoed weakly.

"I gave him the number before we went out on our date, just in case anything happened and they needed our help. He put the call through before you headed for the hospital."

Devlin took his place on the other side of Val's bed. Her eyes immediately brightened as he flashed her a greeting.

"Ready for the big performance, Val?"

She shook her head and he threw her a mock frown.

"Come on, don't give me that. We've been practicing this for a long time. I say you're ready to meet the little guy who's so eager to come into the world."

Val began to pant under the onslaught of another contraction. Once it had passed, Devlin congratulated her, but when the nurse needed to reattach the blood pressure cup to Val's arm, Michelle pulled Devlin aside, giving them as much privacy as the room would allow.

"Devlin, I'm sorry," Michelle whispered.

He grinned. "About what?"

"You know." She wished he wouldn't make her spell it out to him. "I said some awful things to you this morning."

"Funny, I don't remember any."

"I accused you of putting my kids in danger."

"Did you?"

"Of consorting with my mother in her plots against me."

"Really? I don't remember that, either."

"I told you to get out of my house."

"That sounds vaguely familiar, but I haven't moved anywhere."

Michelle stared at him, oblivious to the curious eyes all around them.

"But you left."

"I didn't leave. I had your mother drop me off at my own place so I could get my car, that's all."

"But—"

He tipped Michelle's chin and forced her mouth to close.

"I figured you needed some time alone to cool off, but that was the only concession I was willing to give you. We still had a lot to talk about."

"Like what?"

"Like my apology for going along with Maude's charade."

"You couldn't have known she would be so devious."

"No, but I should have suspected as much."

"I don't blame you."

"Good, because I also wanted to tell you that you were right. If someone at Worthington was in danger, you deserved to know about it."

"Oh." She couldn't think of anything else to say.

"But there were other more personal things I intended to discuss as well."

"What sorts of things?"

"I think we should get married for one."

"You do?" The words were barely audible.

"Yes. I love you and I know you love me, so I think it's the responsible thing to do."

Her breath locked in her chest. "How do you know I love you, Devlin?" she asked, her words barely audible.

"Because you told me so in your sleep, over and over again."

She flushed when the doctor snickered, then she shifted uncomfortably, even more embarrassed when she realized that they'd been overheard.

"We need to set an example for our teenagers," Devlin said, modulating his voice into an even softer whisper.

"*Our* teenagers?"

"They need to know that there are plenty of happy, healthy relationships in the world and that ours is one of them."

"I agree."

There was a beat of silence, then his brows rose. "You agree?"

"Yes, I do."

"So you'll marry me?"

It was the first time she had ever seen him look unsure and vulnerable.

"Yes, Devlin Rhett, I'll marry you."

A muted round of applause came from the direction of the group surrounding Val. The nurses were dewy eyed, the doctor grinned broadly, and even Val had paused from her breathing exercises to clap.

But when another contraction occurred, it was back to business as usual as Val began to groan.

"Well, if that's all taken care of, you two," the physician said, motioning for Michelle and Devlin to return to their stations, "I think it's time we delivered a baby, don't you?"

LESS THAN AN HOUR LATER, Michelle stepped into the waiting room and slid the cloth cap from her hair.

Everyone was there. Maude and Gerald, Wilson and Frieda, and her kids, all of them. She felt the lump in her throat grow another size. After witnessing the birth of Val's baby and accepting Devlin's proposal, she hadn't thought that she could be any happier. But she'd been wrong. So very wrong.

"How is she?" Annie breathed, rising from one of the plastic chairs.

"Fine. She's tired, but the delivery was normal. Her parents are with her now. They also brought along a visitor."

"Elliot?" Sammy asked, her eyes shining.

Michelle nodded. "There's still some tension between them all, but they felt that Elliot should be here."

"What about the baby?" Pete demanded.

The door behind Michelle opened without a sound and Devlin entered, a small squirming bundle cradled in the crook of his arm.

"Val has asked me to do the introductions. Everyone, this is Rhett."

"Rhett?" Willie repeated.

"Val decided to name her baby after our butler?" Manuel asked in confusion.

Michelle shook her head, wrapping her arm around Devlin's waist. "No," she answered with infinite tenderness and love. "She decided to name her baby after my husband-to-be.

The teens jumped to their feet, gathering around them, peering at the baby and thumping Devlin on the back. Michelle laughed, enjoying it all, knowing that there would be plenty of time for Devlin and her to enjoy one another privately and to repeat their avowals of love. There were plans to be made and adjustments to be endured, but rather than dreading such formalities, she looked forward to each detail.

After all, they both had a lifetime awaiting them.

The butler.

And his bride.

BRIDE'S BAY RESORT

UNLOCK THE DOOR TO GREAT ROMANCE AT BRIDE'S BAY RESORT

Join Harlequin's new across-the-lines series, set in an exclusive hotel on an island off the coast of South Carolina.

Seven of your favorite authors will bring you exciting stories about fascinating heroes and heroines discovering love at Bride's Bay Resort.

Look for these fabulous stories coming to a store near you beginning in January 1996.

Harlequin American Romance #613 in January
Matchmaking Baby by Cathy Gillen Thacker

Harlequin Presents #1794 in February
Indiscretions by Robyn Donald

Harlequin Intrigue #362 in March
Love and Lies by Dawn Stewardson

Harlequin Romance #3404 in April
Make Believe Engagement by Day Leclaire

Harlequin Temptation #588 in May
Stranger in the Night by Roseanne Williams

Harlequin Superromance #695 in June
Married to a Stranger by Connie Bennett

Harlequin Historicals #324 in July
Dulcie's Gift by Ruth Langan

Visit Bride's Bay Resort each month wherever Harlequin books are sold.

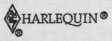

HARLEQUIN ®

BBAYG

HARLEQUIN®

Don't miss these Harlequin favorites by some of our most
distinguished authors!
And now, you can receive a discount by ordering two or more titles!

HT #25645	THREE GROOMS AND A WIFE by JoAnn Ross	$3.25 U.S./$3.75 CAN. ☐
HT #25648	JESSIE'S LAWMAN by Kristine Rolofson	$3.25 U.S.//$3.75 CAN. ☐
HP #11725	THE WRONG KIND OF WIFE by Roberta Leigh	$3.25 U.S./$3.75 CAN. ☐
HP #11755	TIGER EYES by Robyn Donald	$3.25 U.S./$3.75 CAN. ☐
HR #03362	THE BABY BUSINESS by Rebecca Winters	$2.99 U.S./$3.50 CAN. ☐
HR #03375	THE BABY CAPER by Emma Goldrick	$2.99 U.S./$3.50 CAN. ☐
HS #70638	THE SECRET YEARS by Margot Dalton	$3.75 U.S./$4.25 CAN. ☐
HS #70655	PEACEKEEPER by Marisa Carroll	$3.75 U.S./$4.25 CAN. ☐
HI #22280	MIDNIGHT RIDER by Laura Pender	$2.99 U.S./$3.50 CAN. ☐
HI #22235	BEAUTY VS THE BEAST by M.J. Rogers	$3.50 U.S./$3.99 CAN. ☐
HAR #16531	TEDDY BEAR HEIR by Elda Minger	$3.50 U.S./$3.99 CAN. ☐
HAR #16596	COUNTERFEIT HUSBAND by Linda Randall Wisdom	$3.50 U.S./$3.99 CAN. ☐
HH #28795	PIECES OF SKY by Marianne Willman	$3.99 U.S./$4.50 CAN. ☐
HH #28855	SWEET SURRENDER by Julie Tetel	$4.50 U.S./$4.99 CAN. ☐

(limited quantities available on certain titles)

	AMOUNT	$
DEDUCT:	**10% DISCOUNT FOR 2+ BOOKS**	$
ADD:	**POSTAGE & HANDLING**	$
	($1.00 for one book, 50¢ for each additional)	
	APPLICABLE TAXES******	$_____
	TOTAL PAYABLE	$_____
	(check or money order—please do not send cash)	

To order, complete this form and send it, along with a check or money order for the
total above, payable to Harlequin Books, to: **In the U.S.:** 3010 Walden Avenue,
P.O. Box 9047, Buffalo, NY 14269-9047; **In Canada:** P.O. Box 613, Fort Erie, Ontario,
L2A 5X3.

Name: _____

Address: _____ City: _____

State/Prov.: _____ Zip/Postal Code: _____

**New York residents remit applicable sales taxes.
   Canadian residents remit applicable GST and provincial taxes.   HBACK-AJ3

HARLEQUIN®

A M E R I C A N 🔷 R O M A N C E®

American Romance is about to ask that most important question:

Where were you when the lights went out?

When a torrid heat wave sparks a five-state blackout on the Fourth of July, three women get caught in unusual places with three men whose sexiness alone could light up a room! What these women do in the dark, they sure wouldn't do with the lights on!

Don't miss any of the excitement in:

#637 NINE MONTHS LATER...
By Mary Anne Wilson
July 1996

#641 DO YOU TAKE THIS MAN...
By Linda Randall Wisdom
August 1996

#645 DEAR LONELY IN L.A....
By Jacqueline Diamond
September 1996

Don't be in the dark—read
WHERE WERE YOU WHEN THE LIGHTS WENT OUT?—
only from American Romance!

A NEW STAR COMES OUT TO SHINE....

American Romance continues to search
the heavens for the best new talent...
the best new stories.

Join us next month when a new star
appears in the American Romance
constellation:

Liz Ireland
#639 HEAVEN-SENT HUSBAND
July 1996

Ellen couldn't believe her former husband
placed a personal ad for her—her *dead*
former husband! Well, at least that
explained the strange men showering
her with calls and gifts, including
Simon Miller. Ellen was attracted to
Simon—but how was a girl supposed to
start a relationship when her dead
husband kept lurking over her shoulder?

RISING STAR

Be sure to Catch a "Rising Star"!

Look us up on-line at: http://www.romance.net

STAR696

He's at home in denim; she's bathed in diamonds...
Her tastes run to peanut butter; his to pâté...
They're bound to be together

for
Richer,
for
Poorer

We're delighted to bring you more of the kinds of stories
you love in FOR RICHER, FOR POORER—where lovers
are drawn by passion...but separated by price!

Next month, look for:

#640 BLUE-JEANED PRINCE

By Vivian Leiber

Don't miss any of the
FOR RICHER, FOR POORER
books—only from American Romance!

Look us up on-line at: http://www.romance.net

FRFP-2